ELEVEN

TO THE

DOGS

BarbarianSpy

FOR LITERARY HEAT

This book is copyright © habu 2014
habu asserts his right to be known as the author of this work.
Published by BarbarianSpy in 2014
Cover design © S Bush 2014
Cover image: Manipulated: © Jannabantan at Dreamstime.com
ISBN: 978-0-9876093-8-0

BarbarianSpy
Jindalee St
Toronto NSW 2283
AUSTRALIA

ELEVEN

TO THE DOGS

by

HABU

TABLE OF CONTENTS

INTRODUCTION

The guidance given to men seeking a lasting, caring relationship with another man often is to look for a man with a dog. If the man you are considering to do more than just hook up with briefly and casually owns a dog, he is likely to be a patient, caring, unselfish, loyal person, all good ingredients for a serious long-term relationship. He pretty much would have to be to have and care for a dog. Of course a corollary of this guidance is to look for the type of dog he has. If the man has a pit bull, you'd best be shopping for someone who is dominant and forceful; if a Pekinese, you probably should expect to find a sub—and perhaps a somewhat temperamental one.

Among the stories in *Eleven to the Dogs*, you will find stories illustrating just such finds in establishing relationships.

As the guidance is well known, though, you also will find stories here of men who don't actually own dogs pretending they do as a subterfuge for finding the man they want—one looking for men with the patience, unselfishness, and loyalty to own a dog. And gay or not, as these stories illustrate, there is no relationship as strong as that between a man and his dog.

In some of the stories, like "Appalachian Trail" (a young man is lured to the mountains by an older man) and "Oblivion" (the quality of a dog taken to reflect the quality of the man). the use of dogs is incidental to the story. But in some of the stories, including "An End and a Beginning" (a vet responding to the grief of a dog owner), "Always Conditions" and "For the Love of Pete" (young men doing whatever they have to to keep their dogs), and "Der Hund" (a World War I story of saving a dog in the trenches), concern for a dog is central to a budding love story.

Several of the stories are about the use of dogs in a subterfuge to get into a dog owner's pants. "Best in Show" (a mature naval admiral predator going after a show dog owner) and "The Dog Groomer" (a bored husband seducing his wife's dog groomer) take on the theme in a tongue in cheek, humorous way. There is a bit of humor in the playing of "getting to the man through a dog" in "The Personal Attendant" (suborning a dog owner's companion) as well. The theme is played more seriously in "Kennel Opening" (competing with a man's dogs for his attention).

ALWAYS CONDITIONS

"You said you wanted to know when the bitch dropped them. And if you want to see them before I put them down, you'd better get over here fast."

Clyde had jolted Ken out of a deep sleep. It had been a rough day. Classes at the college, followed by football practice. Then he had to stop at the pharmacy on the way home and pick up Laurie's prescriptions and tend to her needs and get a meal ready for her. And then straight over to Clyde's to help with Daisy. She was about to whelp and was having a difficult time with it. He thought Clyde was breeding her too close together. But that was Clyde. Always the bottom line with Clyde.

Ken was in such a hurry to get out of bed and over to Clyde's, up the block from his mom's house, that all he did was pull on his jeans and pause at Laurie's bedroom door to make sure she was sleeping OK before he left.

Good thing he checked, because she had a live cigarette lying on the nightstand. It wasn't close to anything flammable, but one never knew. It was close to an open bottle of bourbon standing on the floor between the bed and the nightstand, though. If the cigarette had dropped in there, chances were Laurie's bed would go up in flames—with her in it.

As much as Laurie demanded of him, Ken wouldn't want anything like that to happen to her. His mom was the only one he had left in the world in the way of family. And family had always been important to Ken.

Laurie coughed in her sleep and turned away from Ken as he stubbed the cigarette out in an overflowing ashtray and picked up the bourbon bottle. He had half a notion to pour it out and tell her in the morning she'd drunk it all. But they couldn't afford it, and Ken knew she'd just open another bottle—or send out for another one. Ken couldn't get the booze for her, but that's what she kept Suzy around for—why she still held onto Suzy as her last friend. She didn't need the friends so much as someone to buy her booze for her.

Ken exploded out of the house and padded up toward Clyde's place along the grass lawns in his bare feet.

Clyde lived in the original farmhouse that had been on this tract of land, where cheap bungalows had been built as close together around the farmhouse as county code would permit. Clyde had kept a sizable chunk of the land running back of his house, though, including the original barn area, where he'd installed fenced pens and a couple of dog runs. He had pens inside the barn too, and an office.

Clyde bred Labrador Retrievers. And Ken had been helping him part time since he was a junior in high school. Ken had been there when Daisy was born, and she was his favorite of all the Labs Clyde kept.

Clyde wasn't big on affection with his dogs—for him they were just dollar signs—or debits. When they got to be debits, he had them put down. He wasn't sentimental about them. Half the reason Ken stayed with Clyde was because he didn't want that to happen to Daisy. When she came close to that, Ken wanted to be there to tell Clyde he'd take her, which would be less trouble to Clyde than putting her down.

Ken had tried to provide the dogs with what Clyde wouldn't. Clyde worked him hard in the few hours he paid him for, but Ken had stayed on for extra hours and given the dogs exercise and affection. Daisy had been the one that returned the most affection to him.

When it was time for Ken to go away to college, he'd had several options, having been a state standout on the football field and an outstanding student as well. But there were impediments to him leaving home. It was just him and his mother—had been for years, his father having died in a trucking accident on a snowy mountain road—and his mother was plagued with illnesses real, imagined, and self-induced and was incapable of taking care of herself. She also was a holy terror to anyone else who tried to help her other than Ken, which was one reason her circle of friends was down to just Suzy, who wasn't the sharpest knife in the drawer and would just as easily accidentally kill Laurie as keep her going. And another big reason Ken couldn't leave for college was Daisy and the other Labs at Clyde's.

Ken knew if he didn't help give the dogs at Clyde's some attention and affection, no one else would. Ken even could have gotten some better jobs, ones with better pay and better hours. But then there wouldn't be anyone to help take care of the dogs. And Ken liked working with the dogs.

As fast as Ken had rocketed out of the house and displayed his running skills in covering the distance between his house and Clyde's at three in the morning, he wasn't in time. Daisy was already dead when he got there.

She'd whelped five pups, two of them stillborn, in a wrenching delivery during which she hemorrhaged so much blood that she had lost the ability to sustain her strength.

Ken found her lying on a gunny sack in one of the pens in the barn, all five pups around her. She was alone. Clyde was off in another part of the barn, running water into a galvanized tub the size of a small bathtub.

Ken knelt beside Daisy and ran his hands across her cooling body. He lowered his face to her neck and cried. He'd seen dogs die here before at Clyde's. But none of them had been Daisy. Daisy had been born the first day he'd come to work for Clyde, back when he was barely out of elementary school and felt he needed a job because his father had just died. It was the first day Ken had seen the wonders of another living being coming into the world. He'd followed her all through what was an entirely too short life. She had been bred too close together. He knew that.

"Sorry, Daisy," he mumbled through his tears. "I should have been here. Oh, god, I wished I had been here." He sniffed and then continued, "But don't you worry. I'll take good care of your pups."

That's when he looked up to see that Clyde was reaching down and had the tiniest of the pups, the runt, by the scruff of the neck, was lifting it from where it had instinctively been trying to find a nipple, and carrying it toward the tub of water.

"What? Whatayer doin', Mr. Snepp?"

"Putting them down. They've got to be put down."

"No! Why?"

"There's no bitch around ready to take them on. They have to be put down."

"No, no, you can't. Please."

"I'm not taking care of them," he said. And with the hand he wasn't holding the new-born puppy with Clyde put a hold on Ken's shoulder and let it move down to where he was palming Ken's shoulder blade.

That was when Ken realized he had only come out in jeans. The palm of Clyde's hand on his back felt hot, and at the same time Ken felt shivers radiating out from between his shoulder blades and down his spine. He could tell by the look Clyde was giving him that this had not been a good idea. Not a good idea at all. Clyde had been increasingly showing interest in Ken—the kind of interest Ken didn't want shown to him by Clyde, although he'd been doing so ever since Ken had turned eighteen.

There was a time when Ken had substituted Clyde as a father figure, when Ken's life at home was rotten, and he needed someone to confide in. Then Clyde had been all sympathy and compassion. That hadn't been the real Clyde, though. Clyde had been interested in being more than a father to Ken even then. And Ken had let slip what his interests and inclinations were. And this had fit into Clyde's plans perfectly. Ken had even told him about Lawrence—the friend who lived further up the block and who had gone through school with Ken and then enrolled in the same local college and played on the same football team.

All of this telling Clyde his secrets had been a bad mistake. Not that it was a mistake that Ken had Lawrence—but that it dovetailed so well with the desires and plans that Clyde had of his own. If it weren't for the dogs—especially Daisy—needing Ken, he would have left Clyde's employ—and plans—a year ago, when Clyde first made it clear that he wanted Ken to sleep with him.

"Please, Mr. Snepp. Please. You can't. These are Daisy's pups. We can't."

"I don't have the time or inclination to take care of them and wean them, Ken. It's got to be done."

Ken looked behind Clyde and saw the tub of water and knew what that was for.

"No, you don't have to, Mr. Snepp. Daisy was good stock—so was the sire, General Crisp. They can pay for themselves. The pups can pay out. I . . . I'll take care of them. I'll wean them."

"You don't know what you'd be signing up to, Ken. They'd have to be fed every couple of hours for weeks. You'd have to be here almost constantly."

Ken felt Clyde's hand on his back tremble a bit when he said that.

"You'd have to be here frequently in the day and than a couple of times at night, too," Clyde said as he hunched down more over Ken and his hand slid down Ken's spine and his fingers went under the waistband of Ken's jeans. Ken heard the intake of breath when Clyde discovered Ken was wearing nothing else under the jeans.

Ken knew the avenue he'd have to take. He'd always known that Clyde could be controlled with the hint of sexual contact. Clyde was a touchy-feely kind of guy, and this hadn't been the first time Ken had Clyde's hand run down his bare back like this. And Clyde could be mean and brusque with the people working for him, but he'd always been nice to Ken—as long as Ken hadn't balked at having Clyde touch him.

"I'll do it, Mr. Snepp. I'll take care of them. I'll make sure I'm here every couple of hours. I'll take care of everything." Ken straightened his back, giving Clyde an eyeful of his well-developed chest and gave him a doe-eyed little smile. He could see that it sent chills through Clyde's body. Ken knew he had won.

"Well, OK. But if you can't keep up with them, they'll have to be put down." He leaned back over and let the runt drop beside its dead mother's body again. "You'll find formula over in the supply room. I don't think you can manage it, but you can try."

"I can. You'll see."

"You'll owe me one, though," Clyde said. "There are conditions that'll have to be met."

"Conditions?"

"Yeah, you'll find in life there always are conditions, Ken. I'll be straight with you. You know I've always been interested in getting a piece of what your friend Lawrence gets, and—"

Hey, there's a car that's pulled up outside, Mr. Snepp, Ken said. A couple are getting out of it. Ken had been saved—or at least given a reprieve. He didn't have to ask what these conditions might be, and he had every intention to avoid them if he could.

"I can manage," he said to Clyde's retreating back, trying his best to exude confidence. Truth was, though, that he didn't have the slightest notion how he would manage. All he knew is that he owed it to Daisy to try to save the pups she'd given her life for. He owed that much to Daisy.

* * * *

"Whateryoudoin' home at this time, Ken? Aren't you 'supposed to be in school?"

"I told you, Ma, I'm taking the semester off."

"Taking a semester off? Coach is letting you do that?"

"No, I told you about that too, Ma. I'm taking time off from the sports too. Coach will take me back, I'm sure." But Ken couldn't be all that sure of that. His close friend, Lawrence, had taken his position on the team after Ken had dropped out. And Ken couldn't be sure he'd get it back the next semester, even if he could get back on the scholarship. And if Lawrence liked it at that position, Ken wasn't sure he wanted to take it away from him again.

"Why'd ya do that?" Laurie asked. "School don't suit you? You was so high and mighty about that. And you was goin' a get a great job and take care of me. You find it too much to chew off?"

"No, Ma, I told you. There's a litter of pups I have to get weaned up at Clyde's. He was going to put them down—Daisy's litter—and I promised I'd take care of them. But that means I have to be up there and feed them and clean up after them every couple of hours. So, that and taking care of you means I've had to put school aside for a semester."

"That Daisy. She was the only one you could talk about," Laurie snorted. She turned the volume of the TV down a bit with her remote, took a puff on her cigarette, coughed, and put the cigarette in the ash tray on the table next to her La-Z-Boy. "You would'a thought you were shackin' up with her or something. You and that dog. And what do ya mean havin' to take care of me? Don't you go blamin' your wantin' to drop outta college on me. I can take care of myself."

He didn't tell her that his intentions to avoid Clyde's conditions had run out just the night before, when lights had gone on in the house as Ken had done a 2:00 a.m. feed, his mother having been dead to the world and not knowing he'd been slipping out at need to feed the pups.

Clyde had come into the barn in just his sleeping pants and with a blanket over his arm that he spread over a couple of bales of hay while he was telling Ken in no uncertain terms that the pups would be put down the next day unless Ken gave into his conditions right then and there. Again Ken had come down just in his jeans, and while he was still trying to sweet talk Clyde out of his "conditions," Clyde pushed Ken's back down on the covered hay bales and was unzipping the jeans and flaring them out to expose Ken's dick. Ken moaned and buried his fingers in Clyde's hair as Clyde worked up the dick with his mouth.

Clyde was good as sucking and when he rolled Ken's pelvis up and moved his mouth down to Ken's hole while pumping Ken's cock with his hand, Ken came quickly. Then he just laid back and whimpered, having no will to fight it as Clyde coaxed his thighs apart and moved his hips between them. The first thrust was hard and deep, and Ken involuntarily arched his back toward the floor at the far end of the hay bales. Clyde's powerful chest followed him down, and Clyde's lips and teeth went for Ken's nipples as the older man pumped Ken hard and deep and fast—giving Ken less time to adjust to the cock inside him than Lawrence gave him. As anxious as Clyde had been to do it, it was all over in just a few minutes. Clyde turned and flipped his sleeping pants over his shoulder and was heading back up to the house with no further word to Ken.

Ken lay there, dazed, for several minutes more. Clyde didn't last like Lawrence did, but while he was in there he churned harder and faster. And from what Clyde was mouthing and the grunts and groans he was making during the fuck, Ken knew this wasn't the last time Clyde would want him.

15

"Sure, Ma. I left some dinner for you in the microwave," Ken said in answer to Laurie's question. "I've got to get up to Clyde's for a feeding of the pups."

"Well, don't forget to drop by the drugstore on the way home and pick up my prescription—and at the gas station and get a carton of Virginia Slims. I'm about out, and they've got the best price in town."

"Yes, Ma, I'll do both of those things."

"And the Laundromat. Did you get the wash back you put in the machines this morning?"

"Yes, Ma. I've already brought those home. Folded and in the drawers."

"Well, then . . ." The volume went back up on the TV. "Grab me a Coke from the frig on your way out."

"Sure, Ma. Coming right up."

Ken hoped he could get in and back out at the kennel before Clyde even knew he had been there, but he was out of luck with that.

"Not a bad job with these pups," Clyde said from the doorway to the barn. And he said it with a bit of admiration in his voice. "I sure as hell didn't think you could manage. But you did. Another couple of weeks and they'll manage on their own."

"Yep, it looks like all three will pull through," Ken said. He was busy petting the runt, a male he'd named Dusty, and exercising him by making him follow his hand with his nose. This one had had the toughest time to survive—and it had been the one Clyde had picked up to drown first that panicked night. So, naturally it was the one Ken was attached to the most and also the one that gave him the most loving in return. He'd named the female Daffodil, to complement Daisy, although of course he quickly went to calling her Daffy. And the other male he'd named Dexter, although he felt he might as well have called him Dopey, as this was the slowest of the pups to pick up anything—but the quickest to the food and bottle. And, of course, he was the biggest and the most robust.

"Well, I guess they'll turn out OK," Clyde said. "The two biggest there should be worth something. The runt, though, I don't know."

Ken pulled Dusty to his breast protectively. "Dusty's the smartest of the bunch, Clyde. He'll do fine."

"Well, I don't know," Clyde answered.

Ken thought that no time to ask was better than now—now when Clyde was actually acknowledging that Ken had made something worthwhile of not putting Daisy's pups down. And he'd been thinking about it for some time. What he made from Clyde was just about enough to keep a puppy—so he asked.

"You want one of the pups?" Clyde asked.

"Yes. I figure leaving you with two you weren't counting on should be enough to justify me taking one," Ken said. "So what do you say?"

"I guess it would be possible to do that," Clyde said after glowering a bit and looking like he'd given it some thought. "But not for free, of course."

Ken was afraid of this. It was with a bit of trepidation that he asked. "How much, Clyde?"

"Doesn't have to be a 'how much,'" Clyde said softly, coming closer, crouching down by Ken's side, and putting an arm around his neck. "It can be more like how often. You know what I want. I've told you what I want from you. I liked it last night; you've got such a nice, sweet little ass that I've been thinkin' about it all morning. Give it to me twice a day when I want it, and I'll give you one of the pups."

Ken shuddered and looked up into Clyde's face, trying to keep his composure. "How much in money, Clyde?"

Clyde paused, not appearing to like how the conversation had been deflected. "$800, Ken. These are purebred Labs, Ken, and they've already taken a good bit of my feed. I'd get $1,200 for one on the market. I can't just give one away. Is what I really want that much of a deal next to $800? Think about it. Those are my conditions."

"I'll think about it," Ken answered. And he guessed he should think about it. It wasn't like it wasn't the same thing he was doing with Lawrence—although certainly not twice a day. But somehow Ken didn't think it would be the same—as easy—with Clyde. Clyde had a mean streak in him. Ken didn't really want to have a relationship like that with Clyde; the conditions were just too dire for him.

"I'm keyed up, Ken. You done that to me. I'll let you think about the deal but only if you'll put out again right here and now."

The blanket was still on the hay bales, and Clyde pushed Ken down on them on his belly this time and took him like a dog, holding Ken's head down with a strong, veiny hand on his neck. Again a searingly fast and hard and deep first thrust. And this time Clyde was able to pump him a bit longer than the previous night before he ejaculated.

Clyde stood away from Ken when he was done and said, "There that was nice," Again he turned and walked away, adjusting his pants, and left, and Ken, unable yet to move from the position Clyde had left him in, looked over at Dusty, squatting on the dirt floor of the barn. The pup was nosing his muzzle into Ken's hand and licking him and wagging his tail like he was on cloud nine.

"Where am I going to get $800?" Ken thought. But he knew something had to be done. The pups were getting old enough to either sell or turn loose in the general kennel population. Ken had to do something.

Later, he told Lawrence something of his dilemma out in the woods behind Clyde's barn. They had met and driven into the woods there in Lawrence's car and gotten in the backseat and worked the tension out of each other with Lawrence lapping Ken to a mutual release.

Ken was facing Lawrence and using his knees and forelegs on the seat on either side of Lawrence's hips to raise and lower himself on Lawrence's staff, which was considerably longer than Clyde's but possibly not as thick. Ken liked running his fingers through Lawrence's tight, kinky curls and down along the milk-chocolate muscle curves of his lover's well-develop arm and chest muscles. Lawrence was playing with Ken's nipples with his mouth, which Ken found a bit painful after the brutal attention Clyde had given them—but was arousing enough under Lawrence's more gentle touch that Ken didn't want him to stop—while his broad palms cupped, squeezed, and separated Ken's butt cheeks to give Lawrence's cock maximum depth inside Ken.

* * * *

18

"I don't see the problem," Lawrence said as they were finished and Ken felt Lawrence's cock softening inside him—knowing full well that Lawrence would be ready to go again in just a few minutes. "Just give him what he wants. Clyde is old but he's got a good body. And you know what to do with a willing body."

"I don't know, Lawrence," Ken answered. "I don't really want to get into anything like that with Clyde. He scares me a little. And twice a day. He's already fucked me—twice—so it isn't that. It's the being at his beck and call whenever he wants it."

"So, what's the problem?" Lawrence asked.

"He's cruel and twice a day . . . and I'm not at all sure he'll live up to his side of the bargain in the end anyway."

"You take me fine more than twice in a day."

"Yeah, I can feel another one rising even now," Ken answered in a breathy voice.

And there then were no more words beyond "shit" and "fuck" and "yes, like that," for the next half hour, as Lawrence pushed Ken over on his side on the seat, with Lawrence's body cupping Ken's from behind and one of Ken's legs draped over the back of the front driver's seat as Lawrence's cock mined his channel deep and for what seemed like forever.

"He intrigues me," Lawrence murmured after they both had recovered from the heavy breathing from the effort of a second fucking so soon after the first.

"Then you can have him," Ken said. Months later Ken was reminded he'd said this and was to regret that he had. But for now, he knew he had to get back home and make sure his mother had gotten her lunch. And then it was time to check in on the pups again.

"Sorry about taking your position on the team," Lawrence said as he drove Ken out of the woods.

"Someone had to take it," Ken said. "I'm glad it was you." And he was glad for Lawrence. He just hoped there would still be a position for him to come back to when he started back to college in the next semester—assuming the school and Coach would take him back. It had been quite a sacrifice to put school on hold to save the pups—but each time he went to the kennel to feed and groom them, he knew it had been the right decision to make.

Lawrence left him off on a corner two blocks west of his house so that no one would be the wiser what they had been up to. This wasn't a big town. Gay and black on white would be a double-whammy problem here.

As Ken approached the house, he, first, saw the fire engine on his block, and then, as he broke into a run, he saw the ambulance. It was in the driveway to his own bungalow.

They were bringing Laurie out on a stretcher as he got there. The medics were apologetic when Ken identified himself, and they said they were doing all they could. But Ken knew just by looking at his mother that she already was gone—that the fast trip to the ER and pronouncement there were just formalities.

They were very good to him. Let him go along in the ambulance and spent as much time with him as they were with the woman on the stretcher—probably knowing that the living needed them more than the dead did. And Ken spent the entire time with jumbled thoughts on just where he was now and where it could go from here. He was coming up empty on both counts.

* * * *

"Sorry to hear about your mom."

"Thanks, Coach. Say, the team's looking pretty sharp out there."

"Yep. I think we could go all the way this year. Of course it would be easier if you were on the team."

Ken sat up on the bleacher seat from where he'd been sprawled back with his shoulder blades and elbows propped on the bench above it. He'd come out to watch the local college football team practice. He was about to shove off to St. Louis for a special summer job, and if he could get the coach's attention, he wanted to check out what his prospects were for getting back on the team in the fall. The coach had noticed him in the bleachers and had come over to talk to him; he sat down on the next bench seat below Ken and between the younger man's spread legs.

"I don't know. Lawrence is looking pretty good out there," Ken said, torn between wanting the position back and

20

wanting to stay loyal to his boyfriend. Besides, he did think Lawrence was doing a good job at the position he'd had to give up.

"Yes, Lawrence is fine. But he's not as good as you are yet."

"But he might be by fall."

"Yes, he might be by fall."

"So, Coach . . ." Ken paused because what he asked now was really important to him. ". . . So, what are the chances I can get back on the team in the fall if I can get back into the college?"

"Hmmm. That might be possible . . . depending. You're going to be away still when we start summer drills, aren't you?"

"Yes. Yes, I guess I will be. But I think I can be back before the heavy practicing begins."

"Well, it would be a stretch . . . and I don't think I could put you right back on first string. Lawrence is doing me fine. But maybe I could get you back on scholarship and you could move back up. There'd be conditions, of course."

"Conditions?" Ken asked. He looked down and saw that the coach had a hand on his leg.

"Yeah conditions. I know about you and Lawrence . . . and if you were to give me what Lawrence . . ." Coach's hand moved to Ken's crotch.

"You've been balling Lawrence?" Ken exclaimed. It didn't surprise him that Coach leaned in that direction. There had been rumors and Ken had seen how Coach would come into the locker room after practice and watch the guys shower and dress. But Lawrence? Ken now wondered what Lawrence had done to get his position on the squad. Maybe Lawrence wasn't really as prepared to step into Ken's position on game days as Ken thought he might be. But Lawrence was a top. And coach was acting an awful lot like a top now too.

"I . . . I don't know, Coach."

"I was going to say that there could be special consideration if you gave me what you give Lawrence. I could show you a good time," the coach said, giving Ken's cock a squeeze through his jeans material, leaving no doubt what Coach wanted. "I know you are giving it to Clyde Snepp too, Ken. No, no, don't be like that. Just calm down. There are just a few

21

conditions—nothing you aren't doing for others, Ken. But there are always conditions for getting anything you want, you know." Coach's fingers were on the zipper pull for Ken's jeans.

"I don't know," Ken managed to say, sitting up straighter on the bleachers and causing the coach's hand to drop off his crotch. "I'll write to you from St. Louis. We'll . . . see."

Always these conditions. Ken felt his life was beginning to be ruled by conditions. And it was like a vice closing in on him— all of his options being reduced to the same one—with just the name of the guy who wanted him varying from moment to moment.

A whistle blew from the field, and the team was moving into another drill. The coach grunted and stood up from the bleachers. "It could be fun, Ken. And you'd probably get your starting position back in no time. Anyway, think about it. And, again, I'm sorry about your mom's passing. I know it makes it rough on you."

Yes, it made it rough on Ken. It did so partly because it meant he was losing the roof over his head within a week. The rent was due and now the Social Security checks his mother had been bringing in on her own account and her husband's survivor's benefits had dried up. Ken was over eighteen and on his own. It was all he could do to scrape up that $800 Clyde wanted for Dusty and then he'd have to move someplace else anyway. That's why he had taken a summer job out in St. Louis. He'd be working in a training kennel there and hoped to maybe pick up some marketable skills in training service dogs. That would earn him enough money to get back into college in the fall, it would provide him room and board, and, the clincher, they'd said he could bring a dog with him.

The one thing Ken knew was that he wanted Dusty. He wanted one thing he could cling to that gave him loyalty and affection that didn't come with conditions. He'd thought that Lawrence could provide that—but just because the coach was now saying he and Lawrence weren't doing it, didn't mean they weren't, and if Lawrence was messing with the coach behind Ken's back to get his position on the football team, Ken knew he couldn't count on even Lawrence.

Ken climbed down off the bleachers and headed for Clyde's. He had time to put in there and he had his $800 to pay for Dusty.

"Dusty?" Clyde asked. Then he laughed. "No, I don't remember telling you that you could pick which of the three pups you could have for $800. For that you can have Dexter. That one's eating me out of house and home anyway."

"It's Dusty I want," Ken said stubbornly. "All along it's been Dusty we've been talking about. Dusty's the runt. You've never considered him worth anything. It's Dusty. Why do you suddenly value Dusty higher than Dexter?"

"You know why. It's not the money I want."

Ken cast his eyes down at Dusty, who was squirming with delight in his lap as he crouched down. Ken was almost in tears, and he buried his face in Dusty's neck so that Clyde couldn't see the effect this was having on him.

"These are my conditions, Ken. You can have Dusty, and you can have him for the $800. If. If you move in with me—in my bed—but I keep the papers on him. You let me take you down to my basement and bind you and use my toys and you can have Dusty for free, with the papers." Clyde laughed. "I figure after that experience, you'll want me so much you'll just move in here and Dusty won't be going anywhere. Those are the conditions. Or, give me $1,200 and you can have Dusty here, on the spot, complete with papers. Otherwise walk out of here for your summer job and take Dexter for the $800. It's up to you. Pretty good deal, I think. I don't know why you don't jump at it. I know you're doing it with Lawrence. I've seen you off on Larson's lane and doing it in the backseat of his car. And I'm twice as good as he is, I don't doubt."

Clyde knew Ken didn't have $1,200 and couldn't get it. He was surprised as hell that Ken had managed to scrape up the $800.

"Tell you what, you give up the idea of going off for the summer and move in here with me and give me pleasure down in my basement. You satisfy me, and I'll sign over half the kennel to you—on the condition that you continue satisfying me. That would solve all of your problems."

Ken shuddered and stood up, releasing Dusty with great reluctance. Dusty wove in and out of his legs, rubbing against him and pawing at his calves.

"I'll be back at the end of the summer with the $1,200 for Dusty. Take good care of him until then, please."

And then Ken turned and strode out of the barn without a look back. He knew if he took another look at Dusty, he'd start crying. Worse, if he did that, he was afraid he would cave in to Clyde's expanding conditions—all given with every prospect that Clyde would just keep dangling new conditions in front of his face and not honoring them.

* * * *

"You're looking good. By the end of the summer, you'll be able to handle the training all by yourself."

"Thanks, Brad," Ken answered. "You know I won't be staying to the end of the summer, though, don't you? Got accepted back at school, and I'd like to get back in time to try to regain my football scholarship."

"So I've heard," the dog trainer most of the guys working at the St. Louis Service Dog Academy called "Big Guy" said. "Hate to lose you. You've been a big help around here. That's not the only reason I hate to lose you, of course. Ken, I . . ."

Ken moved uneasily from the sitting position he'd taken on the top of the rail fence while he and the head trainer watched Cindy take the Lab service dog Apache through his paces out on the training field. "I've got to go back, Brad. There's something there I need."

"That Lab puppy you've told me about."

"Yeah."

"You know we have a couple of litters coming on in the kennel here. You know you could have one of those."

Ken turned and looked sharply at Brad, waiting for what the "conditions" were, having known for some time what Brad's preferences were and that Brad fancied him.

"And what would I—?"

Brad laughed an easy, open laugh. "No charge. You've earned it. One of the hardest workers I've known, and you came with skills. You'd worked with dogs before."

"Yeah, I've helped raise them to sell. But that isn't anything like you do with them here, Brad—training them as guide and seeing-eye dogs for people who need the help. It's a mighty fine thing you're doing here. And I wish I could stay. Maybe after I've finished college. Maybe Dusty and I will come back then—if you still want to hire me on then."

"Dusty. Is that the pup's name you're going back for?"

"Yes. I raised his mother. And she died having the litter that Dusty was in. I appreciate the offer of one from a litter here, but it isn't just that I want a dog. I want that dog—the runt from Daisy's litter. It's sort of like having Daisy too. I can't really explain it."

"And, you don't really need to explain it," Brad said. "I can understand perfectly."

"Thanks for understanding how I feel about it," Ken responded.

"Anyone who's had dog will understand. But it will be nearly three months," Brad continued after a spell of silence. "You know a dog can grow and change in that time. How will you even know you'd be getting Dusty? From what you've said about the kennel owner, I wouldn't put it past him to pull a switch on you—just out of meanness."

"I'm sure I'll recognize Dusty," Ken answered. "For one thing, he's got a notch out of his ear. I was there when one of his litter mates did that to him. Clyde wanted to put him down again then, but I told him I was the one meaning to buy Dusty and having the notch didn't bother me, so there was no reason why it should bother him either."

"Well, you and your Dusty will always be welcome here, Ken. Don't doubt that. And it's not just because you are a real good worker."

Brad was looking down toward the ground when he said that, but he lifted his head and what Ken saw in his face was raw emotion, wanting Ken to understand. And Ken understood all too well. He'd been fighting the impulse himself for nearly four weeks now. Brad was a great guy, and, despite being so tall and muscular, he was gentle with the dogs in a way that moved Ken to admiration and something else too, something Ken didn't want to think about, didn't want to acknowledge he was feeling. But the look on Brad's face was just too raw, too wanting.

"Think we could get into your room at the bunkhouse without being seen?" Ken asked in a low voice.

"You'd do that?" Brad asked. "You'd let me . . . without anything . . .?"

"I want you, Brad. There's no conditions from me. Just you. Now, if you want."

They fucked languidly for much of the rest of the afternoon on Brad's bed. They disrobed for each other, standing across the room from one another, their eyes glued to the other man. And, when naked, they moved, simultaneously, as if by signal, close together and began running their hands over the other, the breath of both becoming progressively heavier, the touch progressively more intimate. When their mouths met, Brad's hands went to their cocks, holding them together and gently pumping as they swayed back and forth, one unit, until, with a shudder, Ken came. Ken had put a hand down to get the measure of Brad and he moaned and came all the sooner at discovering a cock that justified his "Big Guy" nickname— bigger than either Clyde or Lawrence—or possibly both together.

Brad guided Ken to the bed and laid him down, full prone on his belly, and straddled his hips. He didn't enter him immediately, but ran his hands over Ken's torso and while he slowly ran his cock up and down on Ken's buttocks crack. He held the bulb of his cock at the entrance of Ken's hole, ever so slowly working it in, as Ken gasped and groaned. Ken reached back with his hands and spread his butt cheeks and came up a bit on his knees to present better to Brad. And then there was a long slide deep inside Ken as he panted and moaned and declared that no, he didn't want Brad to stop or hold back.

And then Ken was going to heaven, never having been fucked like that before—never wanting it to stop—and gasping and groaning when it very nearly never did stop.

Later that evening, in his own bunk, reality started to set in. Life was too complicated. Ken couldn't stay here. He wanted to finish college and he still wanted to play football—and he had

26

Lawrence waiting for him back home. Why did life have to be so complicated?

But Ken heard the door squeak quietly on the hinges and the weight of Brad's torso on his and the hands spreading his thighs. And the cock head once again insistently pressing at his hole and then possessing him and beginning its rhythm of complete mastery.

"Sorry, I couldn't keep away."

"Shhh, don't speak," Ken moaned. "Just fuck."

Much later, exhausted, Ken turned his eyes and watched Brad walk away from him in the light of the dawn. A million-dollar man, that. Worth all of that to someone lucky enough to have him. Just if life weren't so complicated.

* * * *

It was Ken's last weekend in St. Louis, and he was all keyed up. His attraction to Brad hadn't waned in the last couple of weeks—it had strengthened. And now Ken was torn by what he wanted to do, what he wanted out of life. He wasn't all that sure that he wanted to return to his college now. There were colleges here too, and Brad, in a last-ditch effort to entice him to stay had said that Ken could tailor his work hours around going to college here and that the training academy would even help with tuition.

The more Ken thought about going back on the football team, the more he was reminded of the conditions Coach had blatantly specified. Clyde was bad enough, always after him. If Ken went back on the team, he'd still have to work part time for Clyde—or for someone else—and he'd have them both at him. Maybe it would be best to just let Lawrence have his position on the team. And to have Coach too.

That seemed to be the real glitch here. Ken had something going with Lawrence. But if Lawrence was giving it to the football coach, where did Ken really fit into that? Dusty certainly wasn't an impediment to coming back. Brad had said Dusty would be welcome here.

Brad, Brad. Everything seemed to be coming back to Brad.

There was just too much of this to think about.

Ken felt he needed to blow off some steam. So, when Brad's assistant, Cindy, said she was driving into town and would be busy for a couple of hours down there on Saturday evening, Ken hitched a ride with her and arranged a drop off and pick up place and time. Brad wasn't at the kennel. He had a bunk room at the kennel, but he lived downtown and hadn't worked this Saturday.

Cindy let Ken off on Manchester Avenue. Ken had Brad's address in his pocket and a general location. Brad had said he lived near the St. Louis University Medical Center. Ken had a vague notion of going to Brad's and surprising him, and relieving this tension that was building up inside him and putting an end to the indecision. But here, on the street, where Cindy had left him off, Ken got cold feet. Instead of walking toward where he thought Brad lived, Ken started off in a tangent direction.

He needed time to think and to gather his wits about him—and maybe a drink or two to steady his nerve and his resolve. This indecision and beating around the bush—not knowing what he wanted, what he should do next—was tearing him apart.

Ken was walking up Chouteau Avenue when he saw a couple of guys dressed out in leathers entering a bar. The side of the bar facing the street had four blacked-out windows with a logo identifying it as Bad Dog.

Prophetic, Ken thought. Dogs had become Ken's life, and here was an establishment that was welcoming him on his own turf—and matching the mood he was in. So he walked into the Bad Dog and up to the bar and ordered a beer. It was a pool hall sort of place, laughter and smoke. All guys, and most of them dressed in leather. The noise rolled over Ken, making him feel protected and unnoticed. So he sat up on a stool at the bar and ordered a second beer.

But Ken wasn't unnoticed. Several of the guys at the tables and playing pool were watching him out of the corner of their eyes and marking him as fresh tail—and inviting.

First one guy and then another were at the bar, engaging Ken in chit-chat conversation and finding anything he wanted to talk about fascinating. Finding chit-chat a good cover for not having to think about what he didn't want to think about, and

28

thinking these were really friendly guys, Ken felt comfortable with them and was happy to talk to them about St. Louis and how it differed from where he came from. And he was happy to let the two guys buy him another beer. And then there were three guys and yet another beer.

And before he knew it, Ken found himself in the alley behind the bar, with the biggest of the guys who had been talking to him backing him up to a grimy brick wall between a set of trash dumpsters, his face leering into Ken's, the tip of a pool stick under Ken's chin and forcing his head back against the bricks, and the other guy's big fist gripping Ken's crotch.

There was a guy on either side of Ken holding his arms up against the brick wall with grips on his wrists, and cutting through the beer buzz he had on, Ken heard one of the guys mutter, "You first, then me. Sam, you'll have to take sloppy thirds."

Ken began to moan as he felt fingers at his belt buckle.

But then he heard a godawful noise that he barely was able to identify as a car horn and the alley was being lit up by the beams of two headlights.

The guys accosting Ken evaporated and Ken sank to the ground, only to feel himself being lifted and being hazily conscious of the concerned face of Brad looming into his vision.

Somehow Brad got Ken out of the alley and into his car, and Ken was only vaguely aware of being taken back to Brad's apartment, a cup of strong coffee being lifted to his mouth by Brad's hands, and being stripped and tossed in the shower and soaked with cold water.

When Ken woke, it was morning, and his head was pounding, but he was conscious enough to know that he had escaped an involuntary assault—if, certainly, not a subsequent deep fuck from Brad—and had been very stupid to allow himself to get into that position.

He knew before he opened his eyes that he was naked and between sheets and felt very warm and content. He felt the pressure along his side and opened his eyes to find that Brad was laying there next to him. He wasn't asleep, though. His eyes were open and were staring at Ken.

"Hey," Ken said in a quiet voice.

"Hey, yourself," Brad murmured.

"My Prince Valiant. You saved me."

"It appears so."

"How did you know I was there?" Ken asked

"I didn't. I go to that bar. I was entering as you were being hustled out the back. It's happened before at the back of Bad Dog's. And there were three of them. So, I thought it best to get my truck on our side. It worked out."

"Yes, it seems to have."

"What were you doing down there?" Brad asked.

"I thought I was coming to see you. But I got cold feet, I guess. I wound up in Bad Dog's just because it was there and I thought a drink would help me get courage."

"And how did that work out for you?"

"Not too well, or pretty well, depending on how you look at it," Ken answered.

"How do you feel?"

"Like a bad dog."

"Anything I can get for you."

"Yes, as a matter of fact. You can get under these sheets." Brad smiled and lifted his body so that Ken could pull the covers out from underneath him and flip them over him.

Then, as Brad rolled over to face Ken and Ken's hands went to Brad's belt buckle, Ken murmured, "Of course I think you'll find I still have cold feet."

"I'll manage," Brad whispered with a husky voice.

* * * *

"You going to call me every fifteen minutes until I've been to the kennel to get Dusty?"

"It depends," Brad said across the miles. "Where are you now?"

"I'm walking down the street," Ken said. "I can see Clyde's kennel now. I should be in and out in the next half hour or so."

"OK, then, if you call me as soon as you're out and have your dog, I won't have to call you again. Have you been to the college to get reinstated in classes and to check on your sports team status?"

30

"No, not yet. I wanted to do this first."

"Sounds like a plan. Call me when you know something about anything. Love you." It came bouncing off the signal towers into Ken's ear. It clutched at him whenever Brad said that. Ken hadn't dared say it back—at least not yet. Or at least not within Brad's hearing. He groped for something to say, but Brad saved him the trouble. He laughed and closed the circuit.

As Ken got closer, he saw a car in Clyde's driveway he didn't expect to see there, and he had half a notion to turn around and regroup, having a good idea what it meant. But he had put this off long enough, so, although he had pulled up short for a minute, he got his rear back in gear and walked down the drive and to the kennel in the old barn at the back. He could hear Clyde whistling happily away as he approached.

"Well, lookie here. Look who's back."

"Hello, Mr. Snepp. I came back for the Lab pup—for Dusty—just as I said I would. And I've got the $1,200 you're asking for."

"Well, now, I thought maybe you'd ask about your job first, sonny," Clyde said as he lowered the sack of dog food he was bringing into the center aisle from the storage room. "Gone nearly three months, leaving me in the lurch for help. And I suppose you thought you could come right back into the picture. Does that mean you've considered my conditions and are ready to play?"

"Let's settle on Dusty first, please, Mr. Snepp. Then, yeah, I'd like to know if the part time job is still open if I can get back into the college. No conditions though, please."

"Well, the job's filled anyway," Clyde said, with a bit of a smirk on his face. "I can't go three months without having the help. And the other position is filled too."

"Well, then, that's OK," Ken said. He looked through the barn door up toward the back of the house. As he did so, he saw a curtain at one of the windows flutter and the hint of a figure there. And he wasn't all that surprised. Disappointed on one level, but for some reason his insides were turning over and he was feeling all excited deep down at his core. Somehow doors were opening for him and possibilities were falling into place—streamlining his life maybe when he had thought it was tied up in knots.

31

"OK, I can live with that," Ken repeated the sentiment. "I'll just settle up with you and take Dusty then and be on my way."

"Well now, that would be a fairytale ending and all that," Clyde said. "But as much as I'd like to take your money, that's not possible. That runt of Daisy's came down with distemper and I had to put him down about a month ago. I might sell you one of the other . . ."

Ken didn't hear the rest. He had sunk to his knees, blood rushing to his eardrums and sounding like a pounding surf. What Clyde had baldly said cut him to the quick. He was taking gulping breaths and had his arms stiffly propping up his torso, ready to faint away dead on the floor.

* * * *

When Ken was able to regain his composure he struggled up from the floor of the barn and started walking—out of the barn, down the driveway, and down the street, toward his home that was no longer his home—trudging like a zombie. Not thinking about anything at all. Still in shock. The tears running down his face nearly blinded him, but he had walked this route so often that he could have done it in his sleep. He almost had done it in his sleep several nights when Clyde had called him in to help with some sort of trouble with the dogs. Like the night Daisy died. The night she whelped Dusty and then died. And the nights he'd cared for her pups.

About half way to the house that no longer was his home, he noticed that a car was driving alongside him slowly—at the same pace that he was stumbling along.

He recognized, first, the car and then the driver. He stopped dead in his tracks and the car stopped too.

"Get in," Lawrence said. "Get in and I'll drive you where you want to go. But get in now. I don't want Clyde to see us."

"No. I don't want to get in, Lawrence. I don't want to—"

"I've got something to tell you. Something you'll want to hear."

Ken stood there for the longest moment, looking at Lawrence. Seething at what Lawrence had done. Even before Ken had left for St. Louis, Lawrence was getting it on with the coach and taking up Ken's position on the football team. Being willing to bottom for men when he was a top just to get what he wanted. And now Clyde. He had betrayed Ken. Had shown he wouldn't be faithful to Ken.

And then Ken's face went red with embarrassment at the realization that he hadn't kept faith with Lawrence either. That he had made love to Brad. And not just the once. So he didn't really have a reason to feel all that betrayed. And it was worse than that. When Ken had seen Lawrence's car in Clyde's driveway and Lawrence slipping behind the curtain in the window of Clyde's house, what Ken had felt was release and relief. He had already subconsciously made the decision he wasn't coming back for Lawrence. And Lawrence had saved him the embarrassment of having to say it.

Ken sighed and walked around to the passenger side of the car and got in.

"Where to?"

"I don't know. I don't really know where I was going. I had planned to go back to the motel with Dusty, I guess, and then over to the college. Don't feel like going to the college now, so I guess it's back to the motel. The one over on Sycamore. You know. The one we went to one . . ."

Ken let it die there. He didn't want to talk to Lawrence about that just now.

"OK, the motel then, I guess," Lawrence said. "Can't go back to my place, because I let that go."

Ken sat there, staring out the passenger wind, not wanting to look at Lawrence's face.

"I let it go because I'm living with Clyde now."

"I figured that," Ken answered, his mind going to having seen Lawrence in the window at Clyde's.

"He needed help and he offered me room and board in addition to pay . . . and . . . a share of the kennel if . . . if . . ."

"I know. Those were the same conditions he offered me," Ken said—still to the window.

"Still going to college but I'm not on the team anymore," Lawrence said. "I sprained my ankle in practice and by the time I could have gotten back on my feet on the field to resume practices, I'd moved in with Clyde. And then I didn't . . . well, you know. You can get your position back on the team now. I don't think Coach was ever happy you weren't in that position." The last two thoughts were more cheerily offered than the explanation that went before it.

"I know Coach's 'conditions,'" Ken spat out. And now he did turn and face Lawrence. "They were the same conditions he offered you and you accepted before I even went to St. Louis, right? Coach told me all about the conditions you were meeting."

"Ken . . . I . . . I . . . don't—"

"You don't have to say anything, Lawrence. I wasn't faithful to you either when I was in St. Louis. I only tell you because we both know where we stand now."

There was a long pause during which Lawrence kept his eyes glued to the road and Ken stared him down from across the wide vinyl bench seat of the old convertible. Then Lawrence said in a low voice, "You came to Clyde's for that Lab pup you had your sights on, didn't you? It wasn't for me."

"Yes, it was for Dusty. How was I to know you were there? But Dusty's dead. And that means there's really nothing else for me to be here for. I can go to college someplace else just as well as here. Right, Lawrence?"

"That's why I followed you from Clyde's, Ken. I didn't want you leaving with what Clyde told me he told you on your mind."

"What do you mean?" Ken asked. He was staring at Lawrence real hard.

"Clyde lied to you, Ken. That Lab pup you want—Dusty—it ain't dead. Clyde didn't have it put down. He sold it. He sold it to an old lady who came looking for a Lab puppy one day last month."

"Sold him? Dusty's alive?" Ken could hardly get the words out through the gasp. And he would have slid across the seat and kissed Lawrence for telling him that if it wouldn't have set back their mutually understood relationship break by a mile.

Ken almost had to beat Lawrence to do it, but before Ken agreed to get out of the car at the motel, Lawrence had promised to go through Clyde's papers to try to find out who Dusty had been sold to.

****

"Her name's Rosemary Temple and she lives over in Glendale," Lawrence reported to Ken over the telephone the following afternoon. "Do you want her address?"

"Of course. And, Lawrence . . . thanks. And let's just leave it at that, shall we? Let's leave it all at that. But thanks for not letting me leave Clyde's thinking that Dusty was dead."

Ken rented a car and took out for Glendale. He was husbanding his money, so he couldn't let this drag on. There was the college tuition money to throw into the kitty now; he could start college later—after he'd gotten Dusty, if the woman was willing to sell him—when he'd gotten a job and Dusty and he had settled down. He didn't have to give much of a thought to where he'd go and what kind of job he'd get. With all connection to Lawrence now gone, there was no reason why he couldn't go right back to St. Louis and take Brad up on his offer to take on both Dusty and him. Everything was falling into place—just as soon as he managed to get Dusty.

But two and a half hours later, Ken's whole world had fallen apart again. He was setting at the curb at the address he'd been given for the Temple woman—and was staring at a house that had been burned nearly to the ground.

He was so emotional and his hands were shaking so much that he had to sit there for more than a half hour trying to pull himself together, not knowing where to go from here.

It was significant to him, even then, that when he was able to take any action at all, it was to call Brad long distance in St. Louis.

"Calm down," Brad said, using the soothing voice he used on the dogs during search dog training when they had gone on overload. "You have options. Talk to the neighbors about what happened and when and where the woman and Dusty went. Check with the nearest fire department; they should know. Have you done either of those yet?"

"No," Ken said with great difficulty, his throat constricted in frustration and worry. "I called you first. I couldn't think of anything but calling you first."

35

There was silence over the line. "Do you want me to come out there? I'll hop the next plane. Just say the word."

"No. No, thanks, Brad. It's just enough for one of us to be calm and to know what to do. I'll talk to the neighbors and then check with the fire department if none of them can give me information."

"Well, call me as soon as you know anything. Don't wait until you've done a lot of leg work. Call me at each new piece of information you pick up. I'll be right here. We can get through this together."

"OK, thanks. I'll start checking in the neighborhood now. And . . . Brad . . . thanks for being there when I called."

"No, Ken, thank you. Thank you for calling me first."

The check with the neighbors led Ken to a convalescent center not more than two miles from the burned home. Mrs. Temple was elderly and had some minor burns and smoke inhalation and was still in rehab. Nobody knew about Dusty, although two of the neighbors were pretty sure that Mrs. Temple did have a dog she'd recently gotten and that the dog had made it out of the fire.

"Yes, Dusty. That was the puppy's name," Mrs. Temple said when Ken tracked her down, sitting under an afghan on the nursing facility's summer porch. "Good thing I had him. He woke me up in time to get out of there."

"Why, yes, he did make it out of the fire. But, no, no, I don't know what happened to him. I was gaga for days afterward, and when I asked they were kind of vague—said he'd probably been taken to the SPCA. None of the neighbors who have visited said they'd taken him in. It's really been too much. I've worried about what happened to him, but I haven't been able to do much more than worry about myself yet, I'm afraid. I'm sorry. Certainly, if you can find him, I'll sign over any rights to him I have to you. I can see that my days of independence are over—I'm not too far gone not to realize that. There will be no place for a dog with me now. But I'm sure happy he was there that night. I sure do hope you find him."

"Stay put," Brad said when Ken called him from the convalescent center's parking lot. "I'll send money if you need some. We can both start calling the local pounds there. Do you

36

need me to send some money? Do you want me to come there now?"

"No, thanks," Ken answered. "It's enough to know you're there when I need you. I might try picking up a temporary job, but I'll be spending time trying to find Dusty through the pounds—and I'll go to the fire department. Maybe someone there took him someplace."

"Well, if you need a job referral, just let me know who to contact. And if . . . no, when . . . you have Dusty, you know you can come here. No strings attached that you don't want attached. No conditions, dire or otherwise."

Ken had been quite open with Brad concerning the pressures he'd gotten from both Clyde and Coach to have sex with them.

"Thanks, Brad. Those are the best conditions I've heard in quite some time."

* * * *

"I'm glad you stopped by. I wanted to get in touch with you. And, oh my, what a beautiful bouquet. Are those for me?"

Ken had settled into a motel and was stopping by the convalescent center to give Mrs. Temple a contact number for him in case she heard any more about Dusty—and he was in luck, she had.

"It was my niece, Anne. They called her as my next of kin when I was brought into the hospital, and she came up from Spring Hill. The fire department turned the puppy over to her."

"So, she—"

"No, I'm sorry, she doesn't have Dusty anymore. She was afraid I'd want to move back into a place of my own and she didn't want there to be any reason I would argue to do that. She's interfering that way—about my only living relative, but I'm glad she's as far away as Spring Hill. It's bad enough having to make decisions like this at the end of life, but it's worse when you have someone standing over you and pushing."

"She doesn't have Dusty anymore?" Ken interjected, not wanting to be impolite but seeking much different information than he was being provided.

"No, I'm sorry, she doesn't. She gave him over to the SPCA down there in Spring Hill. I made her give me a telephone number for the place, though. I had to convince her it wasn't so that I could retrieve Dusty for myself. It's around here someplace. The telephone number, that is. I know it is. Maybe over there on top of the bureau next to the phone. Yes, that slip of paper there, I think."

* * * *

"Hello, Brad? Ken here. I've got some . . ."

"I think I may have located Dusty," Brad said. The excitement in his voice palpable.

". . . information on Dusty. The SPCA in a place south of here—Spring Hill—"

"Spring Hill?" If anything Brad became more excited.

"Yeah. The lady with the burned-out house told me her niece in Spring Hill took Dusty but already has turned him over to the SPCA. I'm about to call them, but I'm too excited to be coherent to strangers, I think. So I've called you first."

"You don't need to bother to call them, I don't think," Brad said.

"Oh? Why? What do you know."

"Well, I know that a Lab named Dusty was at the Spring Hill SPCA. And I know that I can make some calls and get you set up to check the dog out and see if it's your Dusty."

"OK, I'm listening."

"Somebody's already taken the Dusty the SPCA there had—"

Ken groaned.

"No, wait. I think we can work this out if it's your Dusty. The guy who took the dog is legally blind and wanted a dog to be trained as a service dog. Labs are good for that and the SPCA said they'd hook the guy up with a dog trainer if he took the Lab they had. They called me for a reference of someone who could do that in their area—and when they told me it was a Lab named Dusty, I hopped all over the opportunity and gave them your name. The blind guy in Spring Hill will be expecting you to come and maybe train the Lab he's got as a service dog. If it's your

38

Dusty, I'll be happy to give the guy a dog that's already trained to his needs if he'll trade for Dusty. If it isn't your Dusty, you can still consider taking the job of training the guy's dog—he apparently is rich and has accommodations for anyone who will train his dog if they're willing to stay on the premises. You'd be close enough to the area you're in to continue searching for Dusty there. What do you think about that?"

"I think I love you."

The line went silent, and Ken felt the shock of what he had said. He had wanted to say that to Brad for some time now, and something had prevented him from doing it. And this had just burbled out. But this isn't how he'd wanted to say it. He didn't want Brad to think he'd say this because of what Brad was doing to help him find Dusty rather than being something between him and Brad—no strings, no conditions.

"God, I'm sorry, Brad. I didn't mean it like that. It isn't because of what you're doing about Dusty."

"I'll take it any way I can get it," Brad said. And Ken could tell from the sound of his voice that Brad was happy. "And who can do anything but love a man who wants a dog so badly he'll go through what you have to find him?"

* * * *

Ken drove up to the iron gates of an estate in a wooded section of Spring Hill, where houses could barely be glimpsed through the trees from the narrow, winding, oak-lined lane, but where what little could be seen was dripping in money and size.

He rolled up to a box on a pole arcing out to the side of the section of the drive separating the lane from the eight-foot gates suspended between fieldstone pillars with a six-foot stone fence disappearing into fir trees in both directions. He punched the button, and the gates started opening without a vocal challenge. He had called ahead. The voice at the other end of the phone had been soft, cultured, unmistakably male, with a slight southern accent.

As he drove up to the Mediterranean-style stucco house with a red-tile roof and made a swing into the parking apron, Ken's eye was caught by what he saw in a large window to the left of the entrance porch. And his heart fell to his feet. The dog in the window was a Lab, but it was no puppy. It was fully mature and very likely was old. It wasn't barking. It was standing on something inside, its full chest framed in the window, and it was looking warily at Ken, on guard in case its services were needed, but fully in control, showing no sign of hysteria.

Ken almost didn't turn the engine off; he almost just turned the car around in dejection. But he'd called ahead—and the man living here had a different idea why Ken was here than Ken did. There had always been a good chance it wouldn't be Dusty. And maybe there'd be a job here for a while to give Ken a chance to continue his search.

The door opened as Ken reached the top step of the fieldstone entry porch. The man who opened the door was perhaps in his late fifties. He was trim and patrician looking. He had been a handsome man once and was distinctive-enough looking still. He was squinting at Ken, though, and leaning a bit toward him, as if he was trying to locate him, even though Ken stood only a couple of steps short of the double front door. Ken remembered that the man he'd come here to see was legally blind. Strange that he opened his own door in a house like this, however, Ken thought.

"Tim Drayton? Are you Tim Drayton?"

"No, I'm sorry, my name's Ken. I'm here about the service dog training. I called ahead."

"Oh, yes, sorry, so you did. I had thought you were the man they were sending over for the companion position. I thought he was supposed to come today too. But, please, where are my manners? Please, please come in. Two steps in and five to the left, and we'll be in the library. Sorry, my life is ruled by counting steps now, I'm afraid. Oh, and my name is Harold Caswell. But then you probably knew that or you wouldn't have made it here."

Ken followed the man into the library, and as he did so, it clicked with him why the name Harold Caswell had been familiar. This was obviously Harold Caswell the mystery novel author. The library's walls were lined with books and there was a display of Caswell books between bookends on the large mahogany desk that dominated the far end of the room. Two wing chairs were positioned by a fireplace, and Caswell directed Ken to one of these as he lowered his body with a sigh into the other.

The Lab sat in the leather couch in front of the window that Ken had seen him perched on from the outside. His ears were perked up and he was watching Ken closely, and Ken had no question that the dog would intervene if Ken made the slightest threatening move toward Caswell.

Ken was confused. This dog was fully trained. And fully mature too.

"I'm sorry," Ken said. "I was led to believe you had a Lab that needed to be trained as a service dog. Your Lab here—"

"Oh, Sadie? Sadie's here? Come here, girl," Caswell said as he let his eyes scan the room, trying to focus on his dog.

The Lab struggled down from the sofa and trotted over to Caswell's side and pushed its nose into Caswell's lap. Caswell brought his hands in and scratched behind the Lab's ears, and the dog sat down primly—and happily—at her master's side, casting her eyes at Ken with a "didn't you wish he'd do this for you?" look.

"Sadie's my companion dog now. But she's getting on in years, and I thought it was time to let her retire and just be my dog. So, before I lose her services, I thought . . . well, I got another Lab. He should be along . . . ah, I hear him coming now."

Ken heard the woof and was barely able to get half way out of the wing chair when a young Lab bounced into the room and, heading directly for Ken, leaped into his arms with an exuberant bark, and started licking the tears that had instantly appeared on Ken's cheeks. If there was any question that Dusty had forgotten Ken, they were immediately dispelled, although Ken's hand instinctively went to the dog's ear and was rewarded with the feel of a slight notch right where it should be.

Caswell laughed and gazed at the hazily merged vision of man and dog in front of where he sat, while Sadie sat up on her haunches and gave the unwanted puppy a disgusted stare of censure.

"It sounds like my new dog likes you. So, considering the referral I was given on your training abilities, I don't think we really need to spin this interview out," Caswell said, while Ken was doing his best to bring Dusty under control. "You know the salary and offer of accommodations and board while you are here. If they are satisfactory, I'll show you the room you can use—it's really a suite. A mother-in-law's suite, you could say. But I never was in a position to have a mother-in-law. Just a succession of young men using the suite."

As Ken stood and put Dusty down on the floor and tried to keep his balance as the puppy wove in and around his lost friend's legs, Caswell added, "It's not too much to hope for that you can do some cooking, I hope. There's a woman who comes in to fix dinner, but until and unless I can hire a companion, breakfast and lunch . . ."

* * * *

Ken felt like such a coward. It was three weeks later, and still he was playing this charade. Caswell still thought he was here just to train Dusty to be Caswell's replacement service dog, which of course Ken was doing. And, increasingly, it seemed like Caswell thought Ken was falling into the position of being his companion as well. And the longer Ken stayed in the house with Caswell, the clearer it became to him what Caswell really wanted in a companion—and because Caswell was so charming and persuasive, Ken felt himself weakening to him. Perhaps the man's physical impairment had something to do with it, but Ken just couldn't bring himself to be honest with the author on what he was there for.

Almost nightly Ken spilled out his frustration and the feeling of inevitably of spiraling into a long-term position with Caswell—on Caswell's terms—to Brad, who didn't either rail at him or pressure him to get on with the arrangement Brad had offered him.

Throughout it all, Dusty was the ray of sunshine. The puppy reveled in the return of the one he considered his mother—the human who had brought him into the world and protected and nurtured him and who unexpectedly had disappeared from the scene. None of that mattered to Dusty, though, and as happens with dogs, only the joy of the here and now had any effect on him. Dusty was both affectionate and smart, and Ken was having no trouble training him to the duties of a service dog. It wouldn't be more than a month or two before Dusty was trained and whatever relationship that was building up between Ken and Harold Caswell would come to a crossroad.

Caswell made little effort to hide his sexual preferences, and it didn't take Ken long to realize that Caswell's former companion had been more than just that—he'd been Caswell's live-in boyfriend and had left almost in the middle of the night in a snit, with no regrets on Caswell's part except that it abruptly left him without the support staff he needed.

The Tim Drayton Caswell had expected to interview for the companion position had shown up for an interview eventually, but only weeks later. And by that time Ken realized that Caswell had grown attached to him, and the perfunctory interview with Drayton and sending him away signaled to Ken that Caswell had compared the two young men and was pinning his hopes on Ken now—even after Drayton had made clear that he was comfortable with the arrangement being more than that of a companion. Caswell, after all, was a famous author and was quite presentable still. Ken almost felt he was being too picky himself—too selfish on what he wanted in life—and was not taking his opportunities as he found them.

But Ken now knew that what he wanted was Brad—Brad and Dusty. And therein was the rub, because the longer he went without being honest with Caswell, the more Dusty became Caswell's dog—and not just his dog, but his service support as well.

There came the inevitable evening when Ken knew this all was coming to a head—and he hadn't the vaguest notion what he was going to do when Caswell asked him to climb the stairs to Caswell's bedroom.

Caswell had spent the afternoon on the open back porch, with Sadie by his side, listening to and casting a smile at Ken working in the yard with Dusty. Everything about the afternoon was mellow mixed with the anticipation of something important about to happen.

As the afternoon shadows lengthened, Caswell asked Ken to come up on the porch—to open a couple of bottles of fine wine—and to sit with him, Sadie at Caswell's side and Dusty at Ken's and to read back the chapter of his latest book that he had dictated to the secretary who transcribed his writing just that morning.

Near the dinner hour, Ken looked over and noticed that Caswell had nodded off, but as Ken quietly put the book aside and rose to go into the house, Caswell murmured, "Thank you, Ken. You are a true treasure," and Ken went on into the house. As he passed the dining room table, he saw that the best china and silverware were out and candles and a large bouquet of flowers in the center of the table.

All of this was screaming at him Caswell's intent to make this a romantic evening that would end with the two of them in the same bed.

And Ken had no idea what he would say, how he would react. He only knew that he had been weak up to this point. He went upstairs and rang Brad, wanting counsel and support. But Brad didn't answer.

That evening, as the cook brought in the coffee and port and was dismissed for the evening, with Caswell's soft-voiced thanks, Caswell asked Ken to move to a chair closer to him. Ken steeled himself and moved to beside Caswell, miserable in the knowledge that he was so weak in the presence of Caswell, regretting that Brad hadn't answered the phone, and taking that as a sign on where Ken would be sleeping that night.

"I understand now that you didn't come here for me, Ken—that you came here for Dusty."

"Harold—"

"No, no, it's OK. I understand. I admire you for searching for Dusty until you found him. I think Dusty is one lucky being. I had hoped . . . but I see how it is, and I don't want to be an impediment."

"You're no impediment, Harold," Ken said in a low, husky voice. "You've been nothing but kind, and . . ." He couldn't go on. It shocked him, but he found that he was arguing Caswell's case for him now. He was only a simple "yes" now from climbing those stairs with Caswell.

"Nevertheless, I know more today than I knew yesterday."

Ken was confused and his confusion showed in his face. Caswell couldn't clearly see it, but he was holding Ken's hand now, and he could feel it in the touch.

"You have a very good friend in St. Louis, Ken. I understand he's the one who referred you for this job—found Dusty here and referred you so that you could be reunited. He called me and told me much of what you were too polite and kindhearted to tell me. He has made a generous offer to me. He is willing to send me a fully trained service dog if I will release Dusty to you. I have no problem with that, Ken. I only have one condition."

"One condition," Ken thought, snapping into attention, all of his senses focused on that hand that was holding his, the finger stroking the back of his hand. Always conditions, those inevitable condition. But in this case not so dire, and in this case, Ken was much more swayed, conditioned, willing than he had been with Clyde's and Coach's "conditions."

"Yes?" Ken asked, steeling himself for the proposal— afraid that he'd say yes, and that it would probably change his life forever. Seeing Brad becoming more and more dim in his future, and feeling his betrayal of the one man who had moved him to acknowledge his love and who had done so much to support him.

"The one thing I need from you is that you will stay here until the substitute dog is sent out from St. Louis and that you put the dog and me through our paces so that I can adjust from Sadie to the new dog."

"That's it, that's all?" Ken said.

"Yes,"

Relief and gratitude flowed into Ken's body and he wanted to stand and cry out for joy. But he stayed put, because Dusty had sensed the joy in Ken's body and had hopped up into his lap and was licking at his cheeks—a serious break in training for dining room behavior that Ken totally ignored.

"But what about your need for a companion? I can't just walk off and leave you—"

"Oh, I've decided Tim Drayton will be satisfactory after all," Caswell said. "I called him this morning right after your friend called me—and I said yes to your friend already, by the way—and Drayton will be moving in this weekend. You can keep your room; I have someplace else for Drayton to sleep."

Fifteen minutes later, Ken was in his room, still fighting off the affections of Dusty, and dialing to St. Louis. "Brad? Brad,

45

is that you? Send that new dog for Caswell as soon as you can, please. Dusty and I want to come home."

AN END AND A BEGINNING

Prince, the Border Collie, was staring intently up into the eyes of Julien, his master, with a gaze that exhibited a mixture of pain, confusion, despair, and trust. But Julien wasn't looking at him now; he was looking into the eyes of the veterinarian, Troy, with essentially the same mix of emotions in his eyes.

"There isn't . . . ?" Julien started to say, but faltered, not able to complete the sentence.

"I'm afraid not, Julien, not really. Maybe he could go home for a couple of days with enough sedatives so that the pain was minimal. But he'd probably not be able to move. And I doubt he would eat."

"So, you think . . . ?"

"I can't tell you what to do, but if Prince were mine . . ." Troy couldn't complete that sentence. He had treated Prince for the past seven years. Prince was among the first dogs Troy had seen after he'd opened this vet hospital. It was almost like Prince was his. The love of dogs was what had brought Troy to this career—not just dogs in general but each and every one he treated. He swallowed hard. This wasn't about him. This was about Julien. He'd interacted with Julien too for those seven years. And it wasn't about Prince, really. Prince was fifteen years old. Prince was wanting to go; he was begging to go. Julien naturally couldn't see that in Prince's eyes. He was too close to the dog. Troy felt close to Prince too, but he could see it. Prince was ready to go; Prince's concern was for Julien.

"So, if I took him home . . . just for a couple of days . . ."

"There's little chance it would be painless for him or that there's any hope for recovery. He's fifteen, Julien."

"I know . . . but . . ."

"Would you like to go into the waiting room . . . if . . . when . . ." He stopped. He knew what was needed. Prince knew what was needed. But he couldn't be the one to say it or to suggest it. Julien had to accept it. Julien had to say it—or give some sign.

Julien took Prince's paw in his hand. Prince whimpered, lowered his head, and licked the hand.

Troy stood there, watching the man, waiting.

"No . . . I'll stay here. I owe it to Prince. I owe it to Lloyd."

At the sound of Lloyd's name Troy stiffened a bit. Prince had actually been Lloyd's dog. Troy hadn't known that for nearly a year after he'd seen Prince for the first time. It had always been Julien who had brought Prince in. And only Julien long enough for Troy to have developed an interest of his own in Julien. And then he'd learned that there was a Lloyd in the picture. And that Prince had been Lloyd's dog before he and Julien had hooked up. But Lloyd was dead now. Gone for nearly a year. He'd been older and had had a heart condition. Julien hadn't taken it well. He didn't accept the inevitability of it. He wasn't taking this well either.

Well, if it weren't for his professional obligations—and knowing what Prince wanted, needed, Troy wouldn't be taking this any better than Julien was.

"So, you've decided . . . you're giving permission . . ."

"I'll stay . . . I won't leave him until it's over."

When it was over, Julien sank to the floor beside the table, in tears.

Julien called for an attendant, and they both managed to get Julien back to his feet.

"Sam, take Mr. Wilson to . . ."

"I can't go back to the waiting room like this," Julien whispered in a hoarse voice. "It wouldn't do for the other pet owners to see me like this—to think of their own pets in this situation."

"No, certainly not," Troy said. "Sam, please help Mr. Wilson to my office. And get him a cup of coffee."

"No, thanks. I don't need coffee."

"A glass of water then. I'll be in in a few minutes, Julien. After I've . . ."

"I can't have him burned, Troy," Julien said in a panicked voice. "Lloyd wouldn't have wanted . . ."

"No. We'll talk of that later," Troy said. "There are options, and we'll talk about that later. Go on into my office and sit for a while. When you're ready, I'll drive you home."

"But my car? And you have work to do."

"We can get your car back to you tomorrow. And there's nothing I need to do here more than to see you home safely. You needn't hold back with me. I understand."

"Do you? Do you really? He was the last connection I had with Lloyd. Do you really understand?"

"Yes, Julien, I think I do. Prince was special to me too. You're special to me. Go rest a while in my office and then I'll take you home—I have a few things to take care of here and then I'll be with you."

After Julien left the room, Troy wrapped Prince in a receiving blanket and called in another assistant to take the dog from there—the assistant would know what to do.

Then Julien went into an adjacent supply closet, locked the door behind him, sank to the floor, and gave himself ten minutes to control his own tears.

* * * *

"You just sit here on the sofa, I'll get you something from the kitchen. The fixings for coffee easy enough to find?" There were photographs everywhere Tony turned in Julien's house. Nearly all of them were of the three of them—Julien, Lloyd, and Prince. Tony didn't want to see them, but they were everywhere, like this was a shrine. It was bad enough for Julien that Lloyd was gone, but Prince was gone now too.

Maybe that's why Tony wanted to get into the kitchen— maybe there wouldn't be any photographs, two-thirds of death, staring at him. But there was one on the refrigerator, he saw, now that he'd entered the kitchen.

The voice wafted in from the living room. "My car. I don't know . . ."

"I'll come back for you tomorrow," Tony called back. "We'll go someplace where there's a pet cemetery . . . if you're ready to look. Then I'll take you back to where you can pick up your car. I see the coffee maker, but where do you keep your coffee?"

Tony poked his head out of the kitchen. "I don't mean to rush you on the pet cemetery idea . . . maybe you're not ready yet to—"

"I think I'd like that. A cemetery for Prince. The coffee's in the freezer. But there's liquor under the sink. I think I need a slug of something. If you'll join me. Not too early?"

"No. Not too early for me. Not too early at all."

Tony came out of the kitchen with a bottle of scotch and two glasses. Julien looked so lost, hunched there on the sofa. Tony went over and stood by him at the sofa, poured scotch in both glasses, and hand one to Julien. Julien didn't seem to notice he was there.

"Here, Julien. Drink this."

Julien reached out, without looking, coming first into contact with Tony's thigh. Tony shuddered. He ached for Julien. He'd always been aroused by him—increasingly after he'd learned that Julien was living with Lloyd, who Tony had known was gay. And a bottom, like Tony was. He felt jaded, being aroused like this under the circumstances. But he couldn't help himself. And sometimes in grief . . .

Tony reached down and took Julien's hand and raised it to take the glass of scotch. Julien's hand was trembling, but the glass went straight to his lips and was drained within seconds.

"Again, please," Julien murmured. He lifted his face and the expression in his eyes was achingly similar to that Julien had given Tony when they were consulting on the inevitable "what to do" for Prince. He poured Julien another slug of scotch, which was downed almost as quickly as the first one had been. The third one, he nursed.

Tony downed a glass of scotch himself and stood there, not knowing what to do next, knowing what he wanted to do next.

"I don't know what I'm going to do," Julien whimpered. "Both gone. I feel so empty. I just don't know . . ."

50

"You're going to go on," Tony said, sinking down on the sofa beside Julien and taking him in his arms. "They both had a good run, and they both were lucky to have you."

"I just don't know. How to I begin again? Who would ever . . . ?"

Tony quickly downed another slug of scotch and turned to Julien and said, "I would."

The vet already had his hand on Julien's basket and Julien wasn't pushing him away. Instead, he was moaning and responded, hungrily, when Tony came in for a kiss. Tony had Julien's cock out of his trousers and sank to the floor between his knees.

They first fucked right there on the sofa, with Tony sitting in Julien's lap, facing him, and raising and lowering himself on Julien's cock.

Early the next morning, Julien woke to find Tony sitting on the side of his bed, already dressed and putting his shoes on.

"Tony . . ."

"I'm sorry, Julien. It must have been the scotch. I wouldn't have taken advantage . . . for a million years . . ."

"No apologies. The shock of it was what I needed. It had been so long since I'd . . ."

"Not since Lloyd?"

"No. I thought it was over after Lloyd. I thought I didn't need it anymore."

"I'm sorry," Tony repeated.

"I was wrong about not needing it anymore. It isn't even light yet. Do you really have to go?"

"Yes . . . yes, if you'll be OK for a while. I'll be back after lunch to get you—to go to that pet cemetery and then back to your car."

"Prince? Will we be taking him today?"

"If it's not too soon for you."

"No. Not too soon. The sooner we can put him to rest, the better."

"OK, we'll take him with us." Tony stood, but Julien grabbed his arm, his grip strong, painful to Tony. Misunderstanding, Tony looked down and repeated, "I'm sorry, Julien. I got carried away."

Julien was pulling him down, though, and rising to meet him. They kissed.

"Thank you, Tony. I needed that," Julien said after they'd parted.

Tony's answering smile was weak. "I think I needed it more."

* * * *

"This is it," Tony said. "I hope it will do."

They were standing on a hillside, trees around them, but not set too close together. The land was rolling. They were in a small fold in several hills. A smattering of small tombstones surrounded them.

"It's perfect," Julien. "How did you find this cemetery? It's so isolated, but so peaceful. It's just perfect."

"This is my land. I established the cemetery here when I opened the vet hospital. I wanted there to be this option."

"Your land?"

"Yes. My house is just over the ridge there. If this is fine, you can pick out a spot while I go to the car for Prince and the shovels . . . I can, if you don't think you can . . . or want to . . ."

"No. I want to help. I owe it to Prince . . . and to Lloyd."

They stood there, arm in arm, leaning on the shovels for many minutes afterward, Tony waiting for Julien to be ready to go. Eventually, with a little sob, Julien came out of a reverie he'd been in and said, "We can't stand here forever. I guess we'd better go ahead and go. I'd like to be able to . . ."

"You can come back here any time you want," Tony said. "You saw how we got up here. There's no lock on the gate at the entrance. You can just open and close it yourself when you want to come up here. I'd like you to come to the house now . . . if you feel like it."

"Will there be scotch?" They both laughed, nervously, both striving to break the tension.

"There can be if you want."

"Will there be sex?"

This time neither laughed, and Tony paused, before replying. There was a catch in his voice. "There can be if you want."

"I think I do want."

"First I'd like to show you something."

* * * *

"His name is Duke. He's two months old."

They were kneeling over a cardboard box in Tony's garage. A puppy was trying to make up its mind which man's arm it wanted to try to climb up.

"It's a Border Collie!" Julien said. "It's adorable. Is he yours or are you caring for him for a client?"

"He's yours, if you want him."

"Mine?" There was a catch in Julien's throat when he said that and he was frowning. For a moment Tony thought he'd overstepped. "I don't know. Maybe's it too . . ."

"It's not too soon, trust me on that," Tony said. "In each end, there needs to be a beginning. This would be a beginning for you. There's something you should know before you decide, though."

"What?"

"This is a Border Collie, yes, but not just any border collie. Prince is this puppy's grand sire."

"This puppy's from Prince?"

"Two steps down, yes."

"How do you know?"

"I checked the records in my office. Spent all morning tracking this little feller down. If you don't want him, of course, I'll take him. I thought it would help you to maintain that connection you regretted losing."

"No. I'll take him. I don't usually make decisions this quickly. Maybe I should start doing that, though. New beginnings and all that. And speaking of that, are you part of my new beginning?"

"I can be." Tony looked away, not wanting to see what he didn't really want to see in Julien's face—what he was afraid he'd see. "I'd like to be," he went on to say in a small voice.

"It means the world to me that you would do something this thoughtful. I guess I've been living in my own world too long—not aware of what life has to offer."

"I've been here for you for a long time, Julien."

"Do you have a bedroom in this house?" It was almost a whisper.

"Yes, of course."

"Can we go there now."

"Yes, I'd like that. I'd like that very much," Tony answered.

APPALACHIAN TRAIL

I'm not all that sure how I got roped into going to Ken's daughter's place up on Blue Mountain near Front Royal. It was something about the Appalachian Trail, though, I'm sure. We were sitting at the bar at Scotties, a truck stop bar in Opal where Route 17 breaks off east from Route 29, south of Washington, D.C., to go over to Fredericksburg and the Eastern Shore, and Ken mentioned the Appalachian Trail.

"I've always thought it would be fun to hike a section of that," I'd said. "But I haven't gotten around to it yet. There are the mountains right over there, with the trail running along the top of them, and I haven't found time to hike them yet."

"You're probably still hitting the books pretty hard at that college you're going to," Ike, the bartender, had said. "You got no time for hiking."

"Yeah, I guess," I'd answered. "But a guy can waste his time away hitting the books 24/7—and that sometimes just leads to spending all your time working after you're done with college. I've met a lot of guys who have never been up on the Blue Ridge mountains—never having found the time—even though they are right out there where we all can see them."

"Hiking the mountains can be pretty rough," Stan, the guy who owned the gun shop and firing range in Opal said from down the bar. "You look like you could handle it, though. You on the football team over at that college?"

"No," I answered. "We're too small to be in a football league. I wrestle, though—and work out a couple of times a week. And I ride the hills with my bike. When I'm exhilarated, I just have to get out on my bike."

"Yeah, you look like you work out a lot," Ken, who had saddled up to the bar next to me, said. "Lookin' real good."

I didn't know if I was supposed to melt to that or not. Ken had been nosing around me for several weeks now. I'd found this guy's bar only recently. I'd been going into Washington, D.C., to meet guys—there was a somewhat diffuse gay district around Dupont and Logan circles now. There had once been a full-service club on O Street near the southeast Washington waterfront, where the Anacostia flowed into the Potomac, but that had been knocked down when the new D.C. football stadium was built, and no new center of gay activity in D.C. had formed yet.

And Washington, D.C., was a long way to go. I'd hooked up with a couple of young, good-looking guys here at Scotties, so I'd come here when I didn't have time to go into D.C.

It wasn't really my kind of bar for what I wanted, though. There weren't too many young, in-shape guys coming in here. It was mostly lonely truckers who worked the eastern seaboard and local service worker types who could get pretty rough. And older guys, of course. Those guys were always around gawking and doing their wishful thinking thing. That was Ken—two out of three. He was a trucker, kind of a redneck. Hard muscled, but wiry and older, probably in his mid forties. He was uglier than a fence post, and he didn't seem too bright. About all he could talk about was his truck route and sports—and my body. Not at all the kind of guy for a young college student to hook up with.

Whenever Ken came into the bar when I was here, he tried to saddle up to me and bring the conversation around to complimenting me on my body and getting suggestive about going with him.

"You really want to do some hiking on the Appalachian Trail, you should go up to my daughter's place on Blue Mountain one of these days," Ken was saying. "She's got a house right across the road from where it runs by on its way to the Skyline Drive along the top of the Blue Ridge. You could start with just walking a section of the trail there. There are a couple of entrances to it along the road running up the mountain to her place."

"Yeah, that would be an idea," I'd said. I just said it to be polite, though, and those of us gathered around the bar went on to talk about the rain we'd been having leading into October.

"It'll be a great year for leaf watching," Stan said. "We'll have a lot of tourists coming through as early as the weekend to go up on the drive. The show should be spectacular this year because of the rain we've been getting."

"I'd sure like to see that," I said. On hindsight, I guess that's where I made my mistake—giving Ken his opening.

"I'll be up there, at my daughter's, week after next," Ken said. "I'll be dog sitting. Her and her husband are taking a Caribbean cruise, and I've agreed to house and dog sit for them. I'll be having a gathering up there—doing some hunting and some cookouts for neighbors up there I know."

"You've said before that you liked dogs. That's true, ain't it?"

"Yeah, I like them fine."

"So it would be a chance to play with some. You've got some sort of fall break comin' up from college, don't cha, Dan? You could come up for a couple of days and walk a chunk of the trail. Maybe help give the dogs some exercise in the process. There's plenty of room at the house. I could take you up there when I went."

"Yeah, that would be nice," I said. I wasn't really thinking on what he was saying, though. I was giving the eye to a young hunk who had just come into the bar. I was pretty sure I'd seen him at the Sheetz gas station. He was some sort of shift manager there, I thought. He was a real good looker and strutted around like he had something special. And maybe he did. I was surprised to see him in here. Sheetz was nearby, up at the intersection where 17 broke off from 29, so he must know what sort of bar this was.

He was looking right back at me. Showing interest. So, I wasn't paying all that much attention to what Ken was saying.

"I could pick you up at the college next Friday afternoon and take you up there for a couple of days. Four o'clock in the afternoon suit you?"

"Yeah, sure, that would be nice. Thanks," I said, not fully listening to him. My eyes were on the Sheetz guy, who had sat—or, rather, slouched—at a table, with his chair turned sideways, pointed at the bar, his tight-jeans-clad legs spread and his hand on his crotch. He was still staring directly at me and giving a little smile.

When I went over to his table, he said he had a new Camaro I might like to see. And then he asked me if I'd ever been fucked in a Camaro.

After all of Ken's beating around the bush, I found this guy's direct proposition refreshing. "Not until about fifteen minutes from now, if you've got the time and the dick for it," I answered.

He drove me into the car wash building over behind the Sheetz that was supposed to be closed this time of night and shut the line down so we were alone. After he'd sucked me off, he moved over into the passenger seat and I sat on his cock and concentrated on not letting my head bounce off the ceiling of the low-slung sports car.

This had been worth all that time of putting up with Ken trying to zero in on me.

* * * *

"Uh, I'm tired, Ken—and I've had too much beer. If we're going to walk the Appalachian Trail tomorrow afternoon, I need some shut eye. OK?"

"Yeah, sure, we can go on upstairs."

I'd been standing, but I had to sit down again because a couple of the dogs kept weaving in and out of my legs and, in my condition, it was either sit down or fall down. I liked the dogs, though, and they liked getting the pets I gave them.

"You probably need to clean up down here first, though," I said to Ken. "Didn't you say there'd be some families arrive tomorrow morning for a cookout before we hiked?"

"Yeah, maybe, although they may not come before Sunday. They didn't commit to a specific day. We could leave this and clean it up in the—"

"Sure, if it's there in the morning, I'll help you with it. Goodnight." I didn't let him finish his sentence and I was up off the sofa and my feet were already on the stairs to the second floor. I went straight to the bedroom at the end of the hall he'd said I could use and shut and locked the door, thanking the heavens that the bedroom had its own bathroom. I wouldn't unlock the door until morning. The dogs had followed me upstairs and were whining at the closed door. I would have let them in, but I wanted the door locked against a possible visit by Ken and the dogs would have me up several times in the night wanting to go out of the room again.

I could see what Ken was doing—what he wanted. He kept saying without really saying it that there would be families up here with us. But we'd gotten to his daughter's house after he'd taken me to dinner at the Apple House at the foot of the mountain, and his daughter and her family were already gone. There were just two hound dogs here, which seemed happy to see Ken—and, I was glad to see, made up to me quickly.

I guess he thought that if he bought me dinner, I'd let him fuck me all night up here.

The time that any other people—any families—were coming up here was conveniently receding into later days than he'd suggested. If I'd known he was going to get me up here without others around, I wouldn't have come.

He was old, and rednecky, and ugly—and not the sharpest knife in the drawer. There was nothing he had that I wanted. I was into younger, good-looking guys.

He'd tried his best to carry on a conversation with me in the evening, but he finally gave up and found a college football game on ESPN. Neither one of us gave a crap for either of the teams playing, but we were both more comfortable with that to focus on than fumbling at cross-purposes with each other. The beer had been flowing, but I didn't want to get drunk with him. He was one of those bottomless pits who never seemed to get drunk no matter how much he'd had. I'd noticed that down at Scotties.

He must have thought I was getting drunk, though, because he came over and sat close to me on the couch while we watched the game. He had an arm in back of me on top of the couch back. When I felt the touch of his fingertips on my shoulder, I made like I had to go to the can. And when I came back, I made a point of sitting in one of the armchairs rather than back on the couch. It helped that one of the dogs had hoped up on the couch where I'd been sitting and was stretched out there. As soon as I could feign some yawns and remark on what an exhausting week I'd had at school, I escaped to my bedroom and locked the door.

Ken wasn't there the next morning when I got up. He left me a note about having to go down into Front Royal for some groceries and had left some breakfast for me.

When he came back he was all smiles and good humor, saying that we could pick up the Appalachian Trail up here near the house and walk a couple of miles back toward the foot of the mountain and then turn and come back and that this would be a good introduction to the trail to me.

He seemed to have decided I wasn't going to let him fuck me and was making the best of the situation.

We went out on the trail after lunch, and now I was glad I'd come up here. The forest was a riot of autumn colors. And it was so quiet and everything was so lush and dreamy and mysterious that I was almost having a religious experience out here.

As we approached the intersection of the trail with a pathway that Ken said went back to the road and to a parking lot next to the communications towers that were at the very top of Blue Mountain, we heard muffled voices of men. Right where the other trail came in, there were two young men hikers, sort of sitting on large rocks beside the trail.

"We're foreign students taking a year off and hiking the whole way up from Georgia to Maine," one of the guys said when we approached them and struck up a conversation. They both looked like they were fully capable of doing so. Both were muscular and good looking. They were wearing tight T-shirts, with back packs; cargo shorts; and hiking boots, and they seemed oblivious to the chill in the air.

The blond, clean-cut one said his name was Hans, that he was from Amsterdam, and that he was studying to be a doctor. He was the heavier and taller of the two, but was solid rather than fat. The darker-haired one, with a profusion of curly body hair and a heavy five-o'clock shadow was named Alain; he said he was just studying to study. I thought their English was exceptionally good for foreigners. I also thought they were both so sexy looking that I had trouble keeping my eyes off them.

They and Ken took to each other immediately. They told me they were resting from coming off the Skyline Drive portion of the parkway and were looking for someplace to change into warmer clothes as it was getting chilly.

"Hikers usually follow the warmer weather by hiking down from Maine in the fall," Ken said.

"We know that now," Hans said, with a laugh. He was the more jovial and outgoing of the two. He also seemed to be the "take charge" one and the one ready to make an instant decision and get on with it.

"We're from a house just up the trail there," Ken said. "And we're turning back from here anyway. If you want, you could stop at our house and change your clothes there. Maybe take a break from the hike."

"You live together in that house?" Hans asked. He turned to me and gave me a penetrating look.

"We're there, yes," Ken said.

I wanted to correct the impression Ken was giving, but I didn't have a chance.

"Ja, sounds good to me," Hans said.

The three of them turned immediately and headed back down the trail, toward Ken's daughter's house. I followed along behind.

Not far from the cutoff back to the house, though, I tripped on a tree root in the trail and went down hard, twisting my ankle.

The three men in front of me heard my pained grunt when I went down and stopped and turned.

"You OK, Dan?" Ken called back.

"It's my ankle. I may have sprained it."

"Here, let me see," Hans said, and he crouched down beside me and started unlacing my hiking boot.

"We're not far from the house," Ken said. "You think you can make it?"

"I don't know," I answered.

61

"You could go on ahead," Hans said. "I'll look at this. I have bandages in my pack I can wrap it in and we'll be along shortly."

With no more than that, I was alone in the forest with Hans on the Appalachian Trail. He had gotten my boot off and was gently massaging my foot, feeling for strained tendons. He attentions were both painful and sensual. I grimaced. But I also was trembling under his touch. He was a hunk and was overpowering as he leaned over me. He was exactly what I melted to—when I could get it.

"You live with the older man? You go with men?"

"No. I mean, yes," I answered, flustered. His hands on my foot and ankle and massaging up onto my calf was disconcerting. "No, I don't live with Ken," I said.

"But yes you go with men? I saw the looks you gave me and Alain. In Amsterdam we know what those looks mean. We aren't as reserved in Amsterdam as Americans are here. Alain and I have had more trouble with our hookups here than we are used to."

I paused without answering a bit too long. He gave me a knowing smile and moved in closer between my spread legs and let his hand move up onto my thigh.

"Perhaps you go with younger men then Ken? You maybe hook up with other men, Ja?"

"Yes, I go with younger men—when I like them," I answered in a small voice.

"Perhaps you like me, Ja? I am, what you say, hard for you," he said in a low voice. "You go with me? You let me fuck you?"

"Here? Now?" I asked, shocked, but also melting to him. His knowing forwardness was disarming.

"Yes, of course. Off the path, of course, but where is more beautiful for making love than here in the forest? I give you good fuck."

He raised my bare foot to his lips, licked up the sole, and took my big toe inside his mouth. After he had sucked for a moment, he let it free and moved his hands to my crotch. "Let us see what we have here," he murmured.

"You said off the path," I responded in a strangled voice. "Here, anyone could . . . Oh, god!"

He picked me up and carried me downhill from the trail. Within a few yards we were invisible from the trail in the lush foliage. He found a mossy area and lowered me on the ground on my back, stripped off my jeans and briefs, and moved his knees between my legs. He bent over and took my cock in his mouth, and I moaned for him, and, in short order, was begging for the cock—which he was all too willing to provide.

His fucking was straightforward, no-holding-back plowing, as if we were doing the most natural thing that two healthy young people did in the forest. I was completely taken with the matter-of-fact sensuality of it. Just two young, attractive men getting their rocks off on a pleasant afternoon. I rolled my hips up and lifted my legs over his shoulders, both of us taking care with my ankle, even though I now could feel that it had been just a twinge and didn't hurt anymore—well, not much, not enough to interfere with the fuck. As he did me, we locked eyes on each others, enjoying the reflection back and forth of the pleasure we both were having.

After Hans fucked me, we stayed in that position, panting, slowly regaining our breath. I wanted him again, almost immediately. His virility was obvious in how rapidly he was hard again.

He rose to his feet, and extended his hands down to me. "Here, I carry."

"It's OK," I said. "The ankle doesn't even hurt now. I just rolled it, and it's already OK. I can walk on it."

"No, I show you what I like to do with small men like you. You be my baby." He then reached down and pulled me up. He crouched a bit, bending his legs, while he pulled my ass into his crotch and my channel onto his cock again. I wrapped my legs around his waist and nuzzled my face into the hollow of his neck. His hand cupped and spread my buttocks and, while he stood there in the forest with me draped on his hips, he used the strength of his cupped hands on my buttocks to rise and lower me on his cock until both of us had come again.

Then, with me still whimpering my surrender, and following my directions to the side trail that went to Ken's daughter's place, he carried me to the house.

When we entered the house, we found Ken and Alain sitting in the living room, drinking a beer. They both looked at us bug eyed when they realized I was impaled on Hans's cock. The dogs were weaving around Hans' legs like they were unsure that I was OK.

"We were wondering where you were," Ken said. "Is Dan's ankle—?"

"Where is his bed?" Hans asked.

"Upstairs, last room on the left down the hall. Do you?—"

"Come with me, Alain," Hans interjected. "We have need of you too."

In my bedroom, Hans laid me on my back on the bed and then he and Alain whispered to each other as both started to undress. I assumed they were changing their clothes.

I assumed wrong.

When I'd been stripped as well, I was turned and raised to my knees on the bed by Alain, who stood on the floor behind me, his arm wrapped around my belly, holding me up, as he entered my well-lubricated channel strongly with his engorged cock and began to stroke me deep. Hans came around the other side of the twin bed and fed his cock between my lips.

I had two sexy, young hunks going down on me at once. I'd never done this before, but it was highly arousing and I had absolutely nothing to complain about.

Alain was pulling out of me, but then I was being skewered again. He was thicker and was reaching deeper with his cock this time. And now he was playing me, not just fucking me. He'd pull his cock back and punish my prostate with his bulb, and when I was moaning deeply, he'd thrust deep. He'd stroke until I thought we were in a rhythm. And then he'd change the rhythm, keeping me off guard, making me gasp, not knowing what was coming next—except that it would take me to newer heights of satisfaction.

I don't know when I realized it wasn't Alain fucking me anymore. It might have been the stronger grip on my hips—or the bigger hands. But I looked back and saw that it was Ken fucking me, not Alain.

I no longer cared. Ken was a master of the fuck, and he was playing me like I was an instrument made exclusively for his attention. I suddenly realized the advantage older men had. Ken had the experience of knowing exactly what pleased a bottom and brought the most intense pleasure out of them.

He was still fucking me when the two young hikers were gone. He no longer was ugly to me. I wanted to be fucked on my back now, so that I could watch the tight muscles of his chest contract and expand with his stroking and I could reach out and feel the sinews of his lean, but well-defined muscles and the veins sticking out on his arms because they had no fat to travel through.

"You what?" he exclaimed when he'd brought both of us to climax. "You want to do what? You didn't like it? And your ankle—"

"I loved it," I said. "I just have to get on my bike and pump up hills when I'm this excited and exhilarated. And my ankle will be fine; I need to keep it loose. I'll come right back. I want it again—when you get it up again."

"I can get it up for you right now," Ken said, reaching for me again.

"I saw a bike out by the garage. I can use it, can't I? I'll be right back."

"Sure, knock yourself out," Ken said and he rolled over on his back on my bed—and I could see that he, indeed, could get it right back up for me.

I rode across the top of the mountain, back toward Front Royal, climbing a bit to the peak at the communications towers, where I would turn and come back—being sincere that I wanted him again, could hardly wait to get his dick back inside me, playing me like a violin.

When I hit the rise at the communications towers, I saw them—Hans and Alain getting into a sedan that had been parked in the parking lot there. They hadn't been walking the trail up from Georgia. They'd entered the trail at the communications towers—exactly where we had come across them in the first place.

And then what I had fleetingly seen back at the house when they were dressing hit me. Ken had let off fucking me briefly and he turned to them and I'd seen a flash of green.

He'd paid them.

I'd been stupid. It had all been a setup to help Ken get his cock inside me.

I turned and started peddling furiously back to the house. But my pleasure was more important to me than my pride. I didn't fool myself. I was peddling back to get more of Ken's cocking, not to dredge up any scheming that was in the past.

BEST IN SHOW

It was raining hard in Newport. Otherwise Sandy wouldn't have come to his club to do his running that morning. Sandy taught sailing at the nearby U.S. Naval War College, and at his age—he was pushing forty-eight hard—he had to work extra hours to keep in shape. So far, running ten miles a day had helped keep him hard, but Rhode Island wasn't the best place to assume dry days. So, he'd joined a club that had its own indoor track, and that's why he was here this day. It was raining hard outside and it was time for him to run.

But the track was covered with little furry things on leashes. He had turned back to the men's dressing room in disgust, thinking hard on where he was going to go for exercise now. He wondered if going back to the war college campus and fucking that young naval captain's brains out for two hours would off-set a ten-mile run. It was at least worth a try.

While he was changing back into his street clothes and feeling mad at the world and sorry for himself, he overheard the conversation of two of the guys who were just returning from swimming laps in the club's indoor pool.

"So, what's going down on the indoor track?" asked one.

"Dog show," answered the other.

"Oh, that sissy stuff," responded the one. "Owners besotted with their dogs and looking just like them. Total waste."

"Not completely so," answered the other. "Clive Bailey owns last year's champion—probably this year's champion too. And he's no dog face; he's a real looker, and I understand he's the most delicious bottom in Rhode Island. He's got one of those fluffy little things that win so many dog shows—his dog, I mean, not his ass. I think it's a Japanese . . . no, it's a Chinese Crested. A very oriental name his has: Da Mei Yang. It was in this morning's paper. But that Clive, now he's got the most talented ass on the East coast."

The two laughed as they went off to the showers. Nicest ass on the East Coast was what translated to Sandy. Sandy collected nice asses. And he couldn't resist the challenge of having one that others said was the nicest to be had. Speaking of nice asses, though, there was that young naval captain very ripe and just ready for plucking over at the naval college. Sandy dug out his cell phone and started dialing.

He'd had the naval captain meet him down at the boathouse, where he kept a full range of small sailing boats that he used to train these guys in the basics—these guys who'd forgotten all they knew about the basics of sailing because for the last ten years they'd been driving big ships that did everything but wipe their butts for them on automatic pilot.

Sandy had taken the young captain into a lifeboat hanging off the back end of one of the larger sailing boats, and the nice, young, firm piece of tail was bent over the center wooden seat on his belly and was grabbing the gunwales with white-knuckled fists and throwing his head back and screaming his satisfied lust as a crouching and covering Sandy split him from behind with the biggest cock in New England.

With each thrust Sandy thought first just how nice and tight this young sailor's ass was and, second, wondered how it compared with the one those guys in the locker room were declaring was the nicest ass to be had in this region. Long after the naval captain had whimpered his surrender and Sandy's digging cock had delivered the coup de grace, Sandy was resolving he was going to get to the bottom of this Clive Bailey guy—to the bottom and then into the bottom and a good ten and half thick inches farther than that.

He turned the young naval captain on his back on the centerboard and held his ankles up and out and fucked him again. The guy would be begging for another private sailing lesson again the next day. They all did.

Sandy returned to his Brenton Cove cottage after having stopped at a convenience store and bought the morning paper. His cottage wasn't the most luxurious house on the cove—not by a long shot—in fact its low profile and small size, nestled up to his own private dock but hidden from the road by heavy foliage, rendered it almost invisible. But he liked it that way. And in its own way it was more distinctive than any of the hulking wooden waterfront mansions around it. Sandy was quite certain that more future admirals had lost their male cherries and been fucked three ways from Thursday in his bedroom than any of the other houses on the cove could boast.

He settled down in his favorite overstuffed chair, with its wide view of the Newport harbor beyond a bank of sun porch windows, and leafed slowly through the newspaper. There was the report on the dog show and a picture of the champion, Da Mei Yang, but that was the only picture. Not a bad-looking mutt. Sandy read the article very closely; it revealed that Da Mei Yang was being used as a stud for the Bailey Kennels.

A week later, after the submission of voluminous forms and the writing of a hefty check, Sandy answered his door. The man standing on the threshold looked very young—much too young to have already acquired a reputation as a champion bottom—but Sandy had to admit that he was gorgeous and compelling. He could feel that his cock thought that too. He hoped he wasn't being too obvious. All he had on were a pair of running shorts and shoes.

The young man gave him a wondrous smile. He looked like a young Greek god. Dark and heavily tanned and muscled and all white teeth and tumbling black, curly locks of hair. The little ball of fluff he held under his arm that was the celebrated Da Mei Yang was all smiles too. He'd been told why he was here. Sandy was happy to see that his groomer was smiling even though he didn't yet realize he was here for a similar experience.

"Admiral Thompson?" the young Greek god asked with a luminous smile.

"Yes," Sandy answered with a warm, inviting smile of his own. "Here, come through here to the backyard. The bitch is back here. I have her penned and ready for you already."

The Chinese Crested perked up his ears and began to pant in anticipation. Sandy was more than pleased himself with this Greek god Clive, and he was fairly panting himself as he led the groomer and stud through the bungalow and to the backyard.

69

There was a small, newly improvised dog pen just beyond the lattice-covered and grape-vine bedecked patio off the sun porch, on a short grassy area between the house and the start of the pier out into Newport Harbor.

A dog looking somewhat like a Chinese Crested was bounding around the pen and yapping its silly little head off.

With little fanfare, the young man lifted Da Mei Yang over the lip of the pen, and the champion stud bounded out of his arms and into the enclosure. There was little doubt that the immaculately groomed Chinese Crested knew exactly why he was there.

As Da Mei Yang stood solidly in the middle of the pen and stared down Sandy's pooch, Sandy saddled up close behind the dog groomer. The sounds from Sandy's dog turned from ridiculous but noisy yapping to uncertain yipping to whining, and its head descended lower and lower as Da Mei Yang stood there, majestically, staring the other dog down.

Similarly, Sandy had come in very close to the back of the dog groomer as he stood at the edge of the covered patio, but well in the shadows. The young dog groomer felt Sandy's hand on his arm and the older man's hot breath on his neck. He had been attracted to the retired admiral's handsome, square-cut looks and hard, well-taken-care of body from his first look at the jib of the man. He was graying, but only at the temples, and on him it looked good. He had the torso of a mature man, but one who was still solid muscle and who took pride in and much effort on his form. And the dog groomer hadn't missed the bulge in the admiral's basket and the curly salt and pepper hair that cascade up out of the front hem of his low-rise running shorts when he had opened the door.

The young man felt paralyzed as a hand came around and fiddled with his belt buckle. He didn't move, although he was trembling from the feel of those strong fingers on his arm and the hot breath on his neck, as his belt gave way and he heard and felt the unzipping of his jeans.

He had come here to witness the breeding of the admiral's dog by Da Mei Yang. Visual witnessing of the breeding was necessary for the contract to be valid and a fee paid whether or not the admiral's bitch littered. He couldn't miss this. It meant the better part of a k note, which the kennel wouldn't see if the bitch didn't have puppies and no one was there to attest the breeding.

The dog groomer was nonplused with what the bitch's owner was doing to him. He certainly hadn't expected the attention he was getting, but he was being played so expertly and the admiral was so good looking and arousing that the dog groomer was confused—and he was paralyzed. Did he even want this to stop? He had no idea. He was just so surprised and the admiral was such a dominating force. But . . . But . . .

"Uh, Sir. What—?"

"Shush, shush," The older man was whispering. "Just watch the dogs. You must attest. The contract says—"

"Yes, but—"

The man had pulled down the back of the dog groomer's jeans and briefs, and he had the most gigantic of cocks rubbing up and down between the young man's butt cheeks.

"Ah . . . Ah . . . ," the young man was murmuring. The cock was huge and it was tantalizing. The young man felt his legs trembling and his knees going weak at the movement of the underside of the cock up and down on his hole.

"Watch the dogs," Sandy whispered. "Attest to the breeding—"

Sandy's dog was hugging the ground on its belly. It was looking up with its muzzle and it had its teeth bared and was giving a weak growl. But Da Mei Yang wasn't fooled. Da Mei Yang's muzzle was above that of Sandy's dog and the Chinese Crested stud was still staring the other dog down. And his teeth were more strongly bared, and his growl was much more authoritative than that of the other dog. Da Mei Yang was slowly, one step at a time, moving around the side of the other dog. Sandy's dog had to move its head to maintain eye contact, but it did so. It was being mesmerized. Its growls were turning to whimpering.

Sandy had one palm on the young man's belly now and the other one on his throat, pulling his head back. Sandy was kissing the young man on the neck, and the young man was just standing there, his arms drooping at his side, paralyzed by the admiral's power. And he was whimpering too. Just like Sandy's

71

dog, the young man was whimpering softly, lost in the dance of domination—losing the dance of domination.

Da Mei Yang was behind Sandy's dog now, and Sandy's dog was lifting its hind quarters. It was still whimpering, but the instinctive response of its body was totally out of its control. The palm of Sandy's hand had left the young man's belly, and the dog groomer felt wet fingers at his asshole. His ass was being prepared. He whimpered and he involuntarily, instinctively lifted his butt toward the invading fingers.

Da Mei Yang was moving over the hindquarters of Sandy's dog, covering the back half of its body with his chest and belly. Sandy's dog was whining, beaten, bested. The head of Sandy's cock was now at the rear door of the young dog groomer, who was sighing quietly to himself, beaten, bested.

Sandy's dog yelped and writhed under the encasing champion Chinese Crested as it was invaded by a champion cock, while at the same time, the young dog groomer, still standing, but held in the embrace of the older man, felt his ass being entered and conquered and invaded by a master cock. He too yelped and writhed within the embrace of the stronger, dominating breeder. Being split and plowed by a hard, thick, long cock.

The yelps of Sandy's dog turned to whimpers, and its tongue lolled out of its mouth, and its eyes blazed wildly, and Da Mei Yang thrust and thrust and thrust.

"I speak Mandarin," Sandy whispered in the young dog groomer's ear as he thrust and thrust and thrust. "Do you?"

"No," the young man answered through clinched teeth. "Ohhhh, ahhhh, oh my GAWD. Why—? What—?"

"It's your dog," Sandy whispered and then laughed. "Do you even know what Da Mei Yang means in Mandarin?" Thrust, thrust, thrust.

"Ohhhhahhhhhh. Oh, Noooo. Yes! No, no, I don't know what it means." The young man was panting. His knees gave way, and Sandy turned him to a picnic table and laid him down on his back, spread his legs, and thrust inside him again.

Da Mei Yang was having his way with Sandy's dog too. The dog just huddled there, trembling, its eyes begging both for mercy and for more, swimming already in the champion Chinese Crested's millionaire-dollar cum.

72

"Da Mei Yang means 'big beautiful cock.' Whoever bred your dog knew its worth. And do I have a big beautiful cock too, Clive? Am I the best in show too?"

"Oh Gawd yes, oh gawd yes." But then he continued. "My dog? Clive? It's not my dog. I'm not Clive Bailey. I'm just his groomer. He sent me because he was busy today."

Sandy laughed a deep, lustful laugh. Not at all put off. The young guy was luscious. Worth every bit of what he'd had to pay for a stud fee. He dove deep again, throbbing cock plowing undulating ass walls, deep, down, down, down. And the young man yelped and cried for more.

"That's OK," Sandy said, and then laughed again at the totality of the joke. "This isn't my dog, either. I got it at the pound. I even think it's a male. But it's enjoying itself anyway."

And both the dogs and the men fucked on, with Sandy already scheming how he was going to track down and breed the elusive and legendary Mr. Clive Bailey.

DAMNING SECRETS

I hadn't been given time to devise an escape—which was probably the point. I barely had time to roll out of bed, shower, pull on a pair of shorts, and chain Honey to the wall before the knock came at the door. I knew he was coming before I heard the knock, though, because Honey was growling that particular growl she had. And she was baring her teeth. She was straining at the chain, anchored solidly in the wall, as it had to be, as I opened the door.

No preliminaries. I hadn't expected any. Jack was here either to fuck me or kill me—perhaps both. I had been anticipating this. Honey was on her hind legs, pawing at the air, yipping and growling to beat the band. She hated Jack something fierce. She had a good reason to. He always tried to laugh it off, but if Jack could be said to be scared of anything, it was Honey. And at seventy pounds of attack-trained, fierce German Shepherd muscle, Honey was something to be quite afraid of. I often wondered why Jack had put up with her, hadn't just put her down with one shot, as he had no reluctance to do with a man. But he answered that he would never harm an animal, which came across as sort of funny considering what he did—what we did—for a living.

As soon as I opened the door, Jack lashed an arm out, seized one of my wrists, and spun me around, bending and pulling my arm painfully up my back. As the door slammed shut, he pushed me hard against the wall, my cheek hitting the plaster, which took my breath away and made me see stars. Even if he hadn't taken the wind out of my sails, I couldn't have fought him. He was a six-foot-eight, 250-pound mass of muscle, determination, and need. He had told me he was tensed up and needed a good fuck on the phone. So, this didn't come as a surprise.

And I knew exactly why he was tensed up—and what my part in that was. I knew that better, I hoped, than he did.

He grabbed both of my wrists on one strong hand and forced my arms up the wall over my head. I felt my shorts jerked down my hips and they fell to the floor around my ankles.

"Spread 'em," Jack growled, and I barely had time to pull a foot out of the shorts and spread my stance, before he palmed my belly, pulled my hips out from the wall, and was poking between my butt cheeks with his thick and hard dick.

"Jack, please," I whimpered. "Just give me a . . . oh, shit, oh shit, oh FUCK!"

The massive bulb with the thick metal ring in it had found my entrance, and he was forcing himself inside.

My eyes watered and I grunted and groaned, as he got saddled. Honey was growling and barking and lunging at the chain, trying to pull it out of the wall, trying to get at the man attacking her master—just as the man had treated Honey's previous master. But I knew it was of no use. I did what I could to open to him, as he pushed further into me, and then I just worked on controlling my breathing and doing as little moaning and groaning as possible as he pumped me to his ejaculation.

He didn't care if I had one or not—but I did, a full minute before he was finished. God help me, I liked it rough. And I liked it rough from Jack.

He left me and went to the bathroom—he knew where it was—while I pulled my shorts back up and hobbled into the kitchenette, separated from the living-dining area by a breakfast bar. I put coffee on, knowing he'd want some—and needing some myself. Honey went back down on her haunches, not growling now, but very much on the alert, her muzzle turned toward the hallway Jack had disappeared down.

Her growl warned me of his reappearance before he materialized. He settled on a barstool, naked, his body body-builder muscled, his clothes still by the door where he'd dropped them. He wasn't full hard, but he wasn't flaccid either. I knew he wasn't finished with me. I just hoped it would only be another

76

fuck, not what he could do—what he probably would do if he knew everything.

"I suppose you want a cup of coffee," I said as he perched on the barstool. His body was magnificent, even with the two puckered bullet wounds, one in the right torso under his bulging pecs and the other in his bicep on that side. I had often wondered who had been able to manage that. This was something he did to other people—except that when he did it they didn't get up and walk away from it afterward. He was dark skinned. Maybe some Brazilian in him, although I'd never asked. Black, curly hair—a patch of it fanned out over his pecs and then a line descending into his pubes as well. Big hands and feet, low-hanging balls, a cock that wasn't overly long, except in erection, but was challengingly thick. He was still half hard now. I knew he would fuck me again. And, if something worse was coming, it wouldn't come until after that.

"And an omelet. Four eggs. I didn't have breakfast."

Of course he hadn't had breakfast. It was 4:00 in the morning. And I knew—from experience—that he wasn't an early riser if he didn't have to be. We'd lived together for two years—him in bed with me, usually on top of me, pinning me breathless to the mattress as he took out all of his anger at the world with his cock thrusts inside me. Although that had ended more than a year ago. Everything had ended more than a year ago—except that it was now back to bite both of us in the ass.

"An omelet?" I asked. "I suppose you want something in it too." I meant it to be sarcastic. He'd treated me like his maid—his bitch—before too. He had told me I loved being treated that way. As long as he was fucking me totally, I hadn't disagreed with him.

"The works. You make 'em good."

Honey growled, on her haunches, but still straining at the chain, and we both looked at her.

"You could have done me in the bedroom" I said. "No reason to tease her like that."

"I like her to watch. I like to hear her in a frenzy when I'm spiking you. Makes it wilder, don't you think? And it's not her I'm thinking about. Her intensity and bald hatred makes the fuck sexier for me. For you too, I'll bet."

77

I didn't answer. This was so vintage Jack.

"Why did you come?" I asked as I shoveled the omelet onto his plate. I wasn't sure I wanted to know the answer to that, but I was aching to know. "Are you going to kill me? If so, could you leave the door unlocked and phone someone afterward to come get Honey? I know you can't unchain Honey, and I can't stand the thought of her being trapped here and no one knowing."

He took a big bite of the omelet, his eyes boring into mine. He took longer to respond than he needed to. It was so like him.

"The hearing is day after tomorrow. But you know that, don't you?" he said instead of answering me.

"Yes, I know that. That's why you're here . . . because you know I'll have to testify?"

"That and the tension of having it over my head. I had to fuck someone . . . to ease the tension."

"And Phil isn't convenient?" Phil was who Jack had left me for. I'm ashamed to say it wasn't me who broke it up. Jack got Phil, and I got Honey, Phil's police dog. Honey never could abide Jack. Jack treated Phil like shit just as much as he had me. And Phil had taken it just like I had.

"Phil is out of the picture."

"Ah." I was mortified that this pleased me. After everything. I had been more of a prisoner than anything else when I'd been with Jack. "So, you're worried about the hearing?" I asked.

"Shouldn't I be?" Again the piercing look. I knew this was a crucial point. "I shouldn't have told you I did for Harry. They've got nothing else that's conclusive."

Other than the sniper setup when Harry went down, I thought. The caliber of the bullet. The fact that a single bullet did that right between the eyes from where they'd found the sniper nest. There weren't too many shooters who could do that, and the signatures all pointed back to Jack. But, no, he shouldn't have told me that he took down another member of the hit squad, thinking that it had been Harry who had given Jack up to the Iranians for the Salam at-Tarki hit. At-Tarki had been number two in Oghab 2, the Iranian counterespionage agency in the nuclear facilities field when we were doing our best to sabotage their nuclear development. Jack had taken At-Tarki out in Paris. The Iranians had been told it was him and Jack had had to watch his back especially hard since then.

Jack and Harry had never gotten along, and Jack decided Harry gave him up to the Iranians. I knew he hadn't. But there was no way I was going to tell Jack that. And there was no way Jack should have told me that he'd taken revenge on Harry. This wasn't just any hearing, and people like Jack and me—and Harry—weren't just any citizens. If the hearing concluded Jack had taken out one of us, that would be the end of due process for Jack.

"You shouldn't have told me, Jack."

"That's not the point," he countered gruffly.

"You say that you and Phil have split?"

He sat there, staring at me for the longest minute. He hadn't finished his omelet, but he'd done a good job on it. At length, he stood up from the barstool and growled, "Come around here."

"Jack," I said. "Maybe we should go into . . ."

"I said come around here." I could barely hear him over Honey's barking and the rattle of the chain as she tried to get at Jack. I didn't want to vex her like this.

"Be good to me, Jack," I whimpered, as I came around the side the breakfast island.

"I'm always good for you. I know what you want."

He grabbed my wrists and pushed me to the floor, in front of him. His half-hard cock was jutting out at me, and I opened my mouth over it, the metal of his Prince Albert clicking against my teeth as I worked the cock with my mouth. When he'd had enough, he pushed me away from him, back onto my haunches. I stared up into his face, seeing the fury of his determination there.

Did he know, I wondered. Did he know the all of it? "Jack," I started to say, but then I gasped, as he backhanded me across the cheek and I fell toward where Honey was straining at the chain, in a frenzy now, I wasn't quite in reach of her.

Jack leaned down, grasped my ankles, and pulled my legs up to him, hooking my calves on his hips. I arched up on my shoulder blades and cried out, as he thrust his cock inside me, grasped my buttocks, and started to pull me on and off the cock with long, brutal pulls and thrusts. My barking matched Honey's as she strained to get at us. My arms were flung out, my fists grasping tufts of carpeting. I hooked my ankles at the small of his back and hung on for dear life as he plowed me hard and furiously.

I tried to rise up, grasping at his belly. But he didn't stop. He came down on the carpeting on his knees, pushed his thighs under my buttocks, and fucked on, hard and deep. I tried to raise my torso up to him again, but he backhanded me again and I just fell back, trying to relax to more easily take his thickness, whimpering and moaning and taking the hard, thick assault of his cock.

I knew he was going to kill me. I could tell he was from the look in his face. I was the only witness who could do him in at the hearing.

And the irony was that he had every reason to kill me, and he didn't know it. It hadn't been Harry who had fingered him to the Iranians. I had done that. Because he had left me. Because he had gone with Phil. Because he was such an asshole. Because Honey hated him. Because I hated myself for wanting him inside me so much. If he was gone, surely that ache would go with him.

When he was finished, he just stood over me and looked down at me for a long moment. He was standing between my legs. My legs were bent, feet flat on the carpet, but I couldn't close them. Jack had always left me that way, not being able to close my legs.

Then he backed away from me, scooped his clothes off the floor by the door and pulled them on. He turned to me before he left, and said, "There's room on Phil's side of the bed now. Think about the hearing."

"I don't understand why you don't just take me out?" I muttered in resignation to what would be the logical answer to all of this.

"You can't tell why? Because I want you in my bed. I love to fuck you . . . and because I love you. That's why. You mean you can't see that? It took me living with Phil to know I loved you, but you're smarter than me. I thought you could tell."

When he was gone, I rolled over to where Honey was—just a few feet away from where we had been fucking to the tune of her wild frenzy—to where Jack had been fucking me; it had been all I could do to hang on with him. Honey went down on her belly beside me, her whimperings matching mine. She licked my face and then put her muzzle down on my stomach as I stroked her head. I still couldn't close my legs.

The hearing was the day after the next. I knew I wouldn't say anything incriminating against Jack. And that was because the most damning secret of all was that I wanted him. I wanted to be in his bed. I wanted him to fuck me like he just had—again and again. I even melted to the sound of Honey's reaction in the background.

DER HUND

"Can you do something to keep that bloody hound quiet?"

Barnes had had enough. He was trying to get into James' pants, yes, but the howling of that damned dog was driving him to distraction, and it was just that much more than he needed out here in a muddy trench on the Aisne with the Huns singing and shooting off their guns at ten-minute intervals from dusk to dawn to destroy any chance he and his mates had at a good sleep.

"It's because of Elliott. The dog can't understand why he isn't here anymore."

Elliott, Elliott, Elliot. That's all James could talk about since the lieutenant got splattered in three directions by a well-thrown hand grenade. Barnes thought that, with the lieutenant gone, he himself had a chance with the young—what was he?—a lord or something. Leave it to the aristos to stick to their own beyond the grave.

"It's time to let the dog loose then, if he can't reattach his loyalties, Master James. How did Lieutenant Elliott pick him up to begin with? We were on a bloody panicked retreat march all the way from Mons."

"It was in the woods at the Battle of Mons. The dog was draped over the body of a dead Hun and howling. But Elliott managed to coax her away."

"So, it's a German dog. Maybe it's a spy dog. Maybe . . ." Barnes stopped there. He could see that James was tightening up, distressed and displeased by this. "Sorry, sir, it was just a joke."

The reminder of the difference in their positions, even in the trenches, had caused James to square his shoulders away and helped him to dismiss the comment. "She's a British dog now," James said, his jaw set in determination. "We were going mad—all of us. The dog gave us something other than the fighting to concentrate on. Some sense of what it means to be in the human race."

That's not all you found to pull yourself away from the war, Barnes thought. I know that you and Elliott were fucking whenever you could get the chance. And you're a nice little piece, you are. I'd like to fuck you too. I intend to. Intend to give you a little taste of the democratic. Pull you down a notch. It'll be good for you. After this war, things are gonna open up. There's going to be less of a divide in classes then, you'll see. I'm going to fuck you good—if for no other reason than that you give that mutt the lieutenant took off a dead German higher more regard than you do me. Just because I'm a fisherman by trade and you're an aristo lay about—or were until you felt it was your class duty to sign up for the war. Or you were before we were thrown in together in this mess—and no doubt you intend to return to that if you survive this hell on earth.

Barnes knew he was just blowing smoke about the extension of a class divide into the trenches. It was the Jameses and Elliotts of the world who ranked higher here than the bricklayers, even though it was the bricklayers who had more of a feel for a dirty fight like this. And no matter what else, it would be the Elliotts and Jameses who were called by their first names by each other in civilian life and called master and sir, and the farmers and fishermen, like Barnes, who would be summoned by their last names in all circumstances.

His attention returned to the present, though. At least for the moment, the dog had stopped howling. James was holding her close to his chest, and, though trembling—they both were trembling . . . all three of them were trembling considering the circumstances they were in; there were no real differences between one breathing soul and another in a foxhole—the dog was momentarily quiet.

James had such a look of concern—for the dog—and nervous affection in his eyes that Barnes' ire drained from him. Yes, James was quite a delicious piece, and Barnes hadn't had any tail in weeks. James took it, Barnes knew. He'd seen him taking it from Lieutenant Elliott. Barnes was hard just from looking at James and thinking about what he could do with him—what he intended to get from him. It wasn't just Barnes who was randy for it, he knew. James had liked getting it from Elliott well enough. And Elliott had been dead for over a week now. James was ripe for wanting it. Elliott wasn't here to give it to him and Barnes was more than willing to step in to do the honors.

The dog. The dog was key to all of this.

"There, that's better. She has quieted down," Barnes said. "Sorry to have growled about the noise, but it's a bad thing we've got here."

"Yes, yes, I know. But Dog makes it nearly tolerable. There's got to be some form of sanity and civilization that we're fighting for."

"Dog. Is that what you call her?"

"Elliott and I were discussing names for her. But . . . there wasn't time. Elliott . . . well, we never got beyond calling her Dog. And she answers to that."

"She's just a mutt." A mutt, just like me, compared to you, Barnes was thinking.

"Makes no difference. She's affectionate . . . and shows appreciation for any kindness she receives." The dog was sitting up in James' lap, reaching up to his face with her tongue in reaction to his gentle petting. He had a rope around her neck, which he held onto with a hand for dear life to keep her here. She had been snuffling around, looking for Elliott, and no doubt would go over the lip of the trench looking for him if she wasn't restrained.

Barnes wished he could be kissing the beautiful young man's face like the dog was doing. He reached over and rubbed the dog on the ear, and she turned her muzzle to him and licked his hand.

"Yes, I can see that she's affectionate," Barnes said. "You know you can't really keep her for long here in this trench, though."

"She's safer in the trench than out there. And I feel more human with her here. And she's part of Elliott. I mean to keep her until this all ends. Take her back to England."

"You can't take her back to England. You know the odds of doing that, don't you?"

"It's a goal. Do you have a goal, Barnes? If not, what else keeps you going in this hell?"

You can bet your sweet ass, I have a goal, Master James, Barnes thought. You can literally bet your ass on that. I have a goal of just keeping meself alive through this, Master James. And I wouldn't mind keeping you that way too. And I have a goal of giving you a good fuck, yes I do.

He didn't say all this, though. What he said was, "I have a goal to keep me alive—and have a lookout for you too until the end of this."

"Me?" James asked, giving Barnes a searching look—maybe the first close look he'd ever given the man. He was big—tall and broad shouldered—a ruddy complexion and flaming red hair. Heavily muscled, in keeping with a man who worked hard in manual labor. He was ruggedly handsome. James shuddered, realizing he found the man arousing. If anything, more primeval and overtly sexual than Elliott, who had been a bit effete—had been. "You'd have a lookout for me?"

"You can believe it," Barnes said. "I've had a lookout for you for weeks."

James' mind worked on that. Now that he thought about it, it was true. From the time they'd fallen into a reconstituted unit of the British Expeditionary Forces at the Battle of Mons until they had literally fallen into this trench as the maneuvering against the Huns had settled down to trench warfare on the river Aisne, Barnes had been there, helping James avoid disaster and keeping him moving in the retreat from Mons.

"Yes, you're right . . . I . . ."

Whatever James was going to say was rudely interrupted by the burst of a shell very close by that rocked the very walls of the trench and had the two men hitting the dirt, Barnes protectively on top of James, as clods of earth rained down on their heads.

When they came up for air, the two men's eyes were locked on the other's. The expression on James' face was one of surprise and sudden awareness; the expression on Barnes' was undisguised lust.

Their faces slowly moved toward each other, but suddenly James' eyes opened wide and, lifting the empty hand that had been clutching the end of the rope tied to Dog's neck but now no more, cried out. "The dog. Where is she?"

She wasn't anywhere to be seen.

* * * *

"Where is she? Where's the dog?" James was scrambling around along the base of the trench. There was a pile of rubble beside him, dirt and rocks that had been pulled down off the wall by the nearby blast. He was scrabbling at this with his bare hands, evidently from the first instinct that the dog might be buried under the rubble.

"Hold on, sir," Barnes exclaimed, pulling James' hands away by the wrists. "You'll bloody your hands. And there ain't room in that rubble for there to be a dog there. Quiet down so the Huns don't turn their attention here, and I'll take a look see over the rim and see if she bolted out there."

"You'll raise your head to the rim?" James called out in shock. "You can't. You'll get your head blown off."

"Not if you'll go down the trench and make a bit of noise, Master James. To divert any attention the Huns have to give. Well, go on now. If she's out there, don't give her more time to wander off."

Giving him a look of both panic and appreciation, James moved down the trench and started making noise.

Barnes jumped up on a stool positioned at the base of the wall for the purpose and peeked over the top of the trench. He saw a couple of heads lifted over the rim of the German trench, but the German soldiers' attention was focused to where James was raising a ruckus. He had chosen to play a noisy death scene to make the German's feel good about their one-off hand grenade attack. The dog was out there, three or four yards beyond the rim of the British trench, crouched down and trembling with fear.

In a sotto voce, Barnes called out to the dog, trying to get her attention, but the heads of the Germans snapped back in his direction, and he quickly pulled his head down.

He could hear the Germans talking, and he knew enough of their lingo to know they'd seen the dog. He waited, in fear, listening for the shots that would indicate that the Germans would use the dog for target practice. But then he breathed easier when he didn't hear that, but, instead, heard them calling out to the dog, whistling for it, and speaking in tones of encouragement.

He couldn't let the dog return to the Germans. His goal had been to be nice to the dog to get into James' pants. But now he knew he cared for the dog too. He reached for his ration box and took out a hunk of what they had been told was meat. He took the chance of raising his head to where he could see the dog and extended his arm, his hand holding the hunk of meat, over the rim. He whistled for the dog too and added his voice of encouragement to that of the German soldiers'. Any second now he knew he'd feel a bullet—not hear it but feel it hit him. Or he'd see the dog trot back to the side she'd started on. Barnes knew that would break James' heart.

But no bullets came, and the Germans stopped calling for the dog. The dog turned its muzzle toward him and saw the meat. She moved a yard closer to him, but then stopped, in confusion, immobilized by fear.

"*Es ist meine Hund*," Barnes called out. "*Es ist ängstlich. Es ist nur meine Hund.*" He hoped he wasn't speaking German so badly that he wouldn't be understand. He had tried to convey that it was his dog, that it was scared, and that it only was a dog. He knew it was a risk. If the dog was identified as a British soldier's pet, there was every chance that would initiate the target practice that hadn't happened before. But the spattering of German he heard from across the space between the trenches didn't sound belligerent. And they had stopped whistling for the dog when he had started. And no one had tried to shoot off the hand he had extended over the rim of the trench.

James had crawled back. "What are you doing? Is she out there? You can't expose yourself like that."

"Do you have anything that's white that you can lift on your bayonet?" Barnes asked, ignoring the torrent of concerned words James had unleashed.

James pulled out a handkerchief that had been white as recently as two weeks earlier and, his motions showing he was almost numb with fear and concern, stuck it on the bayonet, and raised his rifle over the rim of the trench.

"Ich komme für der Hund. Nur für der Hund," Barnes called out, trying to let them know that he was coming out of the trench only to retrieve the dog, nothing more. Then, with a gulp and a deep sigh—and shaking off the hand that James tried to restrain him with, he hauled himself up onto the rim of the trench.

"Come, girl, come to me," he whispered in a shaky voice. "Nice meat. I have this nice meat for you. You come to me and I'll share my meals with you, fifty-fifty. You want to see James again, don't you?"

Slowly the dog inched toward him on her haunches. Her whole body was shuddering, but her eyes were on the piece of meat.

The whole world went silent in Barnes' head. He was waiting to hear or feel the shot, but there was nothing, not even birds singing. The whole world was silent, holding its breath.

When the dog had come close enough, Barnes grabbed her and pulled her quickly down into the trench with him. As he descended, he felt his bladder give way. He was peeing his pants. But he didn't care. He felt like crying out for joy—the joy of still being alive—and he was noisily gulping in great drafts of air.

He still was listening for the shots, but instead of that he heard clapping and cheering floating over from the German trench—and down the line of the British trench too, where, unbeknownst to him, British soldiers scattered down the line, more thinly scattered than they wanted the Germans to know, had been watching the little drama and were cheering and clapping as well.

He was clutching the dog to his chest, but he felt a weight pushing him down to the ground, covering him, and James' lips on his.

* * * *

They fucked there on the muddy floor of the trench, wildly, noisily. If others along the British line knew what they were doing, they didn't disturb them or try to stop them. The soldiers, to a man, were tired and beyond fear and caring, having faced battle and death—and, perhaps worse, weeks of just waiting for death in the trenches. There was little distinguishing between right

89

and wrong anymore or the need to feed prejudices or to harbor smug attitudes of what any of them would or would not do to make it through the night.

They clutched the dog between them for dear life, but they were clutching each other as well. They fucked in their muddy, stiff-from-sweat uniforms, Barnes sitting on the ground and James sitting in his lap, facing him, their uniforms adjusted just enough for Barnes to have his cock out and James to bare his ass.

Barnes held James close and James raised and lowered his ass canal on Barnes' cock until both had ejaculated in a flood of spent-up cum. Barnes remained encased, however, and, after they'd rested a bit, they fucked again in the same position, this time less frenetically, more languidly. James knew exactly what to do. He and Elliott had done this several times, like this, before Elliott had been killed.

Afterward, night having fallen, James huddled close beside Barnes, watching Barnes tie the end of the rope attached to the dog's neck around James' wrist. "There, now if Ellie is spooked by a blast and bolts, she'll have to drag you with her over the rim."

"I thought you hated the dog, wanted to get rid of it. I didn't know you cared," James said.

"I didn't know I cared, either," Barnes said. "But you were right . . . right about us needing to try to stay human, on an individual scale, through this hell we're in. The German soldiers over there seemed to get it too. Makes you feel that if they left wars to the rabble like us rather than the generals and politicians, wars wouldn't be near as bad as this."

"You called the dog Ellie," James said, suddenly aware that Barnes had done that. "What . . . why . . . ?"

"I think it's a fitting name, don't you? As you said, it was Elliott's dog. I feel now like it's our dog—mine too. But I understand how you feel about Elliott. And I do want to fuck you again. And again and again. I think it will help us get through this. But I'm not Elliott and I don't want to supplant Elliott in your view of things. I want you, if you continue to want me, but because of you and me, not Elliott."

They sat there in silence for a few minutes, Ellie snuffling back and forth between them, showing appreciation that both were petting her, showing her attention, after that wild ride when she was just a warm body trapped between them as they took their pleasure with each other.

"I don't even know your first name," James whispered.

"It's Thomas, sir."

"If you don't mind, I'll call you Tom from now on . . . and you'll stop calling me sir. I hardly think the distinction is appropriate if you are going to have your dick stuck up inside me frequently now."

"Yes . . . I think I'd like that," Thomas answered.

"Which part? Me calling you by your first name or you having that big cock of yours buried up my arse?"

"Both, sir," Thomas answered, and they both laughed.

"And that's the last time you'll call me sir too, won't it be?"

"Yes . . . James," Thomas responded, a smile on his face, joy in his heart. The class barriers already were tumbling away. He didn't have to wait for the end of the war.

"Where are you from, Tom? I've never asked. And what did you do in life before going to war?"

"No you haven't asked. I'm from the port of Weymouth, in Dorset. I'm a fisherman by trade."

"I'm from near there myself."

"Yes, s——." He'd almost said "sir." This wasn't going to be easy for him. Class distinctions didn't erase that easily. "Yes . . . I know. You are from up at Abbotsbury Hall. And Master Elliott, he was from Maiden Abbey, wasn't he? You were childhood friends, weren't you?"

"Yes," James answered sadly. "We'd come all the way from Dorset together. There will be shock when we don't return together. But . . . but you knew who I was and where I was from, and I didn't know about you."

"Yes . . . that's right."

"We'll have to change that sort of thing when we get home, won't we? It will be a whole new world for England, win or lose."

"Yes, I think it will. And, James . . ."

"Yes?"

"I didn't mean it about not being able to take Ellie back to England with you. We'll just set that now as a goal. You can almost see France from Weymouth over the water on a good day. And I've got me a fishing boat waiting for me in Weymouth. We'll get us all home."

"Thanks, Tom. I'd like that. I'd like that a lot. And now do you know what I'd like a lot?"

"Yes, James, I can feel what you'd like now. And I don't see any problem in giving it to you. Giving it to you real good."

FOR THE LOVE OF PETE

Rick didn't like dogs. If he did he would have paid some attention to whether his apartment house accepted dogs before signing a year's lease and painting the living room wall hunter green in anticipation of an even longer tenancy.

His dad knew he didn't like dogs. And he probably had taken the time to discover that there was a "no dogs" clause in Rick's apartment lease.

So, why, Rick wondered, did his dad use the most vulnerable moment of their long and stormy relationship to saddle his son with Pete—or with tremendous guilt if Rick had refused to take him.

"One last thing, Rick," he had said, as Rick dipped his head low to hear what had to be the eleventh last request—none of which had a thing to do with either Rick or his sister, Rachel.

"Sure thing, Dad," Rick had whispered, being quite sure that his dad would come out of this like he'd done several times before and probably would go on ignoring both Rachel and Rick as he had dutifully done since the day their mother had betrayed him and died of cancer.

"Promise me this last thing. I can't go until I know it's taken care of."

"Yes, I promise," Rick said. But the son had no idea what the father was going to say—that he be buried out at the sheep ranch he had loved so much and so hard, certainly more than he'd ever loved another human being, and that had been hard to him in return? Or maybe have his old Jeep bronzed and used as his casket? Rick didn't really care which. His dad had been little more than an inconvenience and nagging guilt of opportunity lost and relationships gone sour for no reason Rick could fathom for more than a decade. And the son's only comforting thought on that failure to bond was that Rick knew he had given it more thought and been more concerned about it than his father ever had.

The father loved his dog more than he loved Rick—or Rachel—or even his wife when she was still alive, Rick would have been willing to bet.

"I want you to promise to take Pete. Not to put him down or send him to a kennel. I want you to promise to give him a home and see that he is taken care of—personally."

That certainly was a bolt out of hell. Rick's dad knew his son's circumstance, living in a small inner-city apartment. Rick's experience with his dad's dog, Pete, was that the hound didn't like Rick any more than Rick liked the dog. Hell, he had growled at Rick and kept his body between the son and the father whenever Rick had checked in on his dad—giving Rick the impression that the dog thought him capable of patricide. Which, at the moment, if his dad weren't already dying, seemed a viable choice to Rick.

"Why, Dad? Why not Rachel? She lives on a big spread. It would be what Pete is used to. He'd adjust so much better . . ."

"He can't stand Rachel. He'd die out of spite," the dad answered. His voice was weak, though. Rick had to lower his head even farther to catch his words.

Why didn't I know this about Rachel and the pooch, Rick mused to himself. And how could Pete like Rachel any less than he liked me? How could anyone have told? Did he put Rachel in the hospital, like he'd sent Rick to the ER with a bite once? Rick realized at that moment that he had almost as nothing of a relation with his older sister as he had with his dad. They hadn't spoken in years—not really spoken, not about anything serious.

That was a depressing thought. Not as depressing and panic edged as the thought of taking his dad's sheep dog in, though.

"Sure, Dad, I'll do that. But there's no reason to be talking about it now. You'll be fine. The doctors said you'll recover just fine."

But the dad wasn't fine. He died no more than an hour later, defying the doctors to the last. On three previous hospitalizations, the doctors had agreed he couldn't possibly survive, but he had. And the one time they said his chances were quite good, he died. Rick decided his dad was perverse that way. He'd been spiting Rick like that for years. And he had died without saying another thing. His last thoughts weren't about the woman he'd lived with for over thirty years or either one of his children—they were about an old sheep dog named Pete.

* * * *

"You can't keep that dog here. You signed a 'no dogs' lease."

"Suits me," Rick answered. "As soon as I get my dad buried, I'll be finding a new home for his dog. Won't be more than a couple of days. Neither the dog nor I can take this arrangement long, so don't worry about him being here next week."

Rick was inching by the apartment super, a stretched muscle-shirt kind of middle-aged guy named Calvin, who was standing out in the center of the hall in front of the entry door. The door to his first-floor apartment was ajar, revealing a bare room looking more like a gym than a living room and with the TV blaring a professional football game. Calvin was a Neanderthal who divided his life between ignoring calls to do repairs in the building, using his gym equipment to keep his muscles popping out, and chasing the younger male tenants. He'd been trying to corner Rick, whose apartment was catty-corner at the back of the first-floor hallway from Calvin's, ever since Rick moved in.

"Besides," Rick turned and said after he'd gotten past Calvin and was sliding down the narrow hallway at the side of the stairs to the upper floors, "the guy in 3B has a yap yap dog that's been going crazy ever since I moved in and you don't harass him about that."

"Yeah, well, that guy is friendly," Calvin said with a grin that more resembled a leer. "He makes it worth my while to have his dog here. If you was to . . ."

"That's OK, Pete here will be out before the 15th. I just need to get my dad buried first."

Rick felt like shooting himself for having given Calvin that opening. The best thing to do with the super was to say as little as possible—certainly not get smart-assed with him as Rick had just done—and stay out of his way to the extent possible. Rick did know what Calvin wanted, and although Rick didn't exactly shy away from getting it on with another guy, he feared Calvin. He was sure the guy had a mean streak—that he could break Rick in two if he wanted to and that he might just look on that as fun. Rick much preferred the corporate types. The ones stepping out on their wives but wanting to keep up appearances. The private little weekends at mountain cabins. And the nice presents.

None of that was going to happen again, of course, until Rick unloaded Pete.

Rick felt a little guilty about doing it, especially as his dad wasn't even under the ground yet and he had made a promise. But the way Rick looked at it, the request had been just one last jab in a combative, mean-spirited life. His dad had thrown him out on his tail the minute Rick had mentioned the gay word and had barely spoken to him in the six years that followed.

Rick had had to pull himself up by himself and get his own education and find his own job and establish his own life in the city—rejecting the rural life on the sheep ranch that his dad had relished and that had killed his mother, worn her down with long years of worry on living and prospering to the next year and pulling her full share in keeping the ranch going.

Rick didn't feel all that forgiving toward his father for that.

Still, he would have felt more guilty if Pete wasn't such a burden. The dog hadn't done anything but whine and snuffle at the door, waiting for his master to arrive and rescue him. And turning on Rick and growling at every move he made. It was a battle just getting him leashed and out into the park to relieve himself a couple of times a day. And the dog should have wanted to cooperate with that. It was a good thing that Rick's work was within a short walk and he could come home for lunch and to struggle Pete out for a walk, or he'd have to clean up a mess each evening when he came home. Several times a day he remembered his dad saying that the dog didn't like Rachel and he laughed at the suggestion that the dog liked him better.

The inconvenience—and the ingratitude of the dog—were already crimping Rick's style, and Pete had only been here three days. And there was Calvin to worry about. Rick didn't like Calvin having anything over his head. Not at all.

When he gave it thought, Rick didn't blame the dog, really—or not much. And he maybe would have blamed and resented him less if he didn't sense that the dog blamed and resented him even more.

The dog was no dummy. He was a purebred Sheltie— related to a Border Collie. And Rick's dad had paid big bucks for him to have a dog to do exactly what Shelties were good for— herding sheep on an open-range ranch. Until he was retired when Rick's dad retired, the dog had been purely an outdoor, open-range work dog, living in the barn and facing up to his routine of sending the sheep out onto the range in the morning, keeping track of them throughout the day, and nipping their heels back to the corral at night. That Sheltie and Rick's dad were more of a devoted couple than his parents had ever been. And Rick's dad paid more attention to Pete, who had to be more than twelve years old and thus in his dotage now, than Rick and Rachel had ever gotten from the sour-tongued, mean-spirited old coot.

Rick couldn't deny, however, that Pete had loved his father unconditionally. Rick wasn't even sure that Pete would outlive his father for long. The dog sat by the door, perking up his ears whenever he heard footsteps out in the vestibule, but quickly realizing it wasn't his master and sadly lowering his muzzle onto his front legs again and, giving a whine, returning to softly crying his grief.

Through some sixth sense the dog had—Rick continuing realizing that Pete was quite intelligent—Rick was sure that the dog intellectually knew his dad was gone. The dog had probably been fully aware of the old man's deteriorating health over the years. The few times Rick had visited the ranch in the past two years—now just a collection of rotting sheds and bereft of its livestock and not even belonging to Rick's family anymore—he had noticed that the dog increasingly had taken on itself the burden of fetching and carrying for the old man and nudging him when it was time for the old man to eat. Rick had gotten the impression that it was truly the old man that the dog was trying to keep going, not prompting him in panic to have the dog's own needs met.

On the day of the funeral, Pete looked like he was steeped in grief, Rick heard howling start up from his apartment as soon as he opened the front door to the busy street.

Rick knew Calvin would be waiting for him in the hallway, fish-eyed and nasty, when Rick returned from the funeral. But there wasn't anything else Rick could do. He couldn't be everywhere at once, and this was one chore he had to do himself. When he had called Rachel, she asked, with a sigh, how much of a check she needed to send to help cover the final arrangements, and he could almost feel her relax into relief when Rick said there had been enough insurance to cover that.

"So, if you can give me some sort of idea when you can make it East, I'll settle on a burial date."

The silence on the phone line was palpable.

"I won't be coming," Rachel said at last. "I know that sounds awful. But there it is. I see no reason to be hypocritical about it." Rachel, the practical one. The hard one. But then Rick didn't really blame her. She'd had to build a shell to survive the life that had been dealt her. And she'd done all right for herself. The two of them didn't see much of each other, certainly. But Rick knew that this was mostly because of the rough life they'd shared under their father's roof. Whenever they met, any chance that they could have enjoyed the visit was wiped out by the memories that crowded in—the wounds threatening to open again. Wounds that they both had worked so hard to close. Things that needed to be said but that couldn't be said.

"That's OK," Rick had answered. "If I wasn't already here, I wouldn't be coming either."

The ceremony was short. Rick's father had no friends—certainly not here in the city. Less than a 100 miles from the ranch, but the ranch and the city might as well have been on separate planets as far as Rick's father was concerned.

Rick had a priest friend, and he was happy enough to come out and say a few words over the grave, especially when, upon going through the desk out at the ranch, Rick had found that his father was a sometimes professing Catholic. But other than Rick, standing off from the grave as it was being filled in, and the pitiful little spray of roses he'd remembered to stop and pick up at the last minute, there was no other evidence that Rick's

98

father had ever lived or had left any sort of positive mark on the world. Rick felt evil, but he gave a little laugh when, standing there, watching the roses get buried under the clods of dirt, he remembered that his father hated roses.

Rick could hear the howling from a block away when he trudged back from the internment. And sure enough, Calvin was waiting for him in the front hall, wearing athletic shorts and a tight tank top and a scowl going from ear to ear.

"I told you about the dog."

"I know. I just buried my dad. I'll work on getting rid of the dog now."

Something in the way Rick said it, a sudden hardness to his voice, made Calvin shut his jaw on the next comment he was going to make and back into his apartment and shut the door.

What Rick had said, the hardness of it, made Rick do a little double take too before he turned, steeled himself, and walked back to his apartment door.

It was the door that Rick noticed first when he entered the apartment. He might have thought that Pete had rabies from the way the dog was flopping all over the living room. Rick had heard the scratching over the howls while he was opening the door, and when he entered the apartment and turned and looked down, he saw that Pete was well on his way to digging through the wood of the door and escaping. Another unpleasant confrontation down the road with Calvin. And all the dog's doing.

"Stop that, you mutt," Rick yelled in exasperation.

But Pete kept on howling and flinging himself around the room and returning to dig at the door.

"OK, OK, I'll take you out to the park," Rick answered, angry and beside himself. He couldn't get rid of this burden fast enough.

When he'd gotten Pete leashed and followed him out the front door, barely able to keep him under control, Rick was surprised that Pete didn't head for the park a block over, which was the only place besides the apartment that Pete knew in this new and strange—and oppressive—environment. Pete was pulling Rick down the street, north rather than south, where the park was located.

It took Rick a few moments to catch on, and even then it was only a hunch. The dog couldn't be that smart, Rick thought. but smart or not, the dog was trying to drag Rick in the direction of the cemetery that Rick had just left.

Resigned, and curious about his hunch, and needing to get Pete out of ear range of Calvin long enough to think about what he'd do with him, how he'd get rid of a dog this old, knowing that he was on the verge of being tossed out on the street himself, Rick pulled Pete over to his car and pushed him into the backseat. The dog seemed less agitated now that something was happening, no doubt, Rick thought, believing that this clod who had kidnapped him had finally gotten the idea that he needed to take Pete home—to his master, who needed him.

While Rick drove, he also began to get calmer—and to formulate and accept the plan of just taking Pete to an animal shelter on the way home. Admitting defeat and bowing to the inevitable. Failing his father once again in the old man's eyes—but, what the hell. What had his father ever done for him?

When they reached the cemetery, Pete bounded out of the car before Rick could get the leash on him and raced straight for the newly interred grave. Rick stood there, in awe, as he watched Pete stretch out full on top of the freshly laid sod on his father's grave and bury his muzzle into the loose soil in a seam in the sod roll.

Rick heard the dog whimpering, but this wasn't anything like the frenzy the dog had gone into in the apartment.

Time dragged on. Rick had no idea how long they were out there—Pete flattened against the grave and Rick standing at the car. Waiting. At length Rick heard stifled sobbing and assumed it was the dog. But he was surprised and perplexed to realize that the sobs were his own. He had let his mind wander. He had thought of the dog, Pete, and the depth of emotion that the animal obviously felt for his father. And he began to think that his father must have had a vein of something lovable in him for a dog to mourn him like this. And then his thoughts went to what he'd found in the desk—discoveries that he had steeled himself against until now, had pretended didn't exist because he didn't want them to exist. Not just the discovery that his father had been a professing Catholic, but evidence as well that he cared for people—had contributed to charities. Had paid for gifts for both Rick and Rachel that they had convinced themselves had come only from their mother. Had paid tuition bills for Rick that he hadn't even realized he had owed. And the packet of letters. The love letters between his parents, his father's words so poetic and loving.

Rick was crying full bore now, grieving belatedly, but grieving still. Not his father's son in that regard. Still able to grieve and to mourn opportunities lost. Not stone-hearted.

He took a handkerchief out of his pocket and was using it to blot the tears in his eyes. Closing his eyes. Wanting to shut the world out; somehow embarrassed that he was standing out here bawling—even though this was the one place where anyone could be forgiven such a lowering of defenses.

He felt a cold wetness at the other hand that had been dangling at his side, and he jerked the hand to the side. But the cold wetness followed the hand, and Rick opened his eyes in time to see Pete nudge his muzzle into the palm of the hand. Rick knelt down and hugged the dog close—the first time Pete had let him anywhere near him—and the dog responded by burrowing his nose into the crook of Rick's elbow.

After several minutes, Rick stood up and opened the door to the backseat of the car and whispered, "Come on, boy. Let's go home."

Pete jumped into the backseat and turned and sat down like a potentate awaiting the start of the parade, and Rick sighed and climbed into the front seat.

* * * *

The transformation in Pete was dramatic. Rick don't know if the Sheltie only needed to assure himself that his father, indeed, was gone or whether he was moved by the son's breakdown at the car in the cemetery and saw something in Rick of his father—or had seen for the first time some affection in the son for the father the dog loved so much. Whatever it was, from the time they drove away from the cemetery, Pete wouldn't leave Rick's side and seemed almost to be wooing him.

Rick and Pete mercifully avoided a meeting with Calvin in the front hall of the apartment building when they returned from the cemetery, but Rick knew it was just a case of putting off the inevitable. But then, at that moment he still intended on finding Pete a new home. Rick just hadn't been able to carry through with his intent on dropping him off at the SPCA on the way home from the cemetery. The man and the dog had bonded in some way there, and Rick couldn't bring himself to be so hardhearted toward Pete with his dad still warm in the grave. He'd give it a few days.

Rick's dad. There was something inevitable in all of this. Rick was thinking more of his dad when he was dead than he had ever thought of his dad when he was alive. And Rick was thinking of him in more than one dimension. Maybe there had been something more than perversity in his foisting of Pete off on his son. Rick could imagine him—still—liking the thought of causing his son concern and making him squirm. But Rick couldn't think of his father doing that to Pete. Rick hadn't been exaggerating when he thought of Pete as the love of his father's life. And thinking on the flip side of the issue—thinking of what was good for Pete as opposed to what was mean-spirited toward his son, Rick had to think that perhaps his dad's final request was intentional. Perhaps he was giving his son a gift rather than a burden. And perhaps he was entrusting Rick with the one thing he loved best. And, just perhaps, he thought, in his last act on earth, he was giving his son something he needed.

These thoughts gave Rick pause, so that when he returned to the apartment, it was with Pete in tow rather than sitting in some SPCA cage.

They stopped at the park so that Pete could relieve himself before they tried to sneak back into the apartment house. And Pete was as good as gold as the two crept into the foyer and slid down along the side of the staircase to the door to Rick's apartment. Pete didn't bark or even whine and he lifted his paws and set them down so intentionally and delicately as they moved that Rick had to stifle at laugh of his own at the image of the two of them sneaking past Calvin's door.

They could hear the TV going full blast inside Calvin's apartment. The Redskins and Cowboys going at each other on the football field, and they could hear the clicking of barbells as well—Calvin working his body as he watched the television. They paused just inside the door to the street and Pete looked at Calvin's door and then up into his new master's face, and Rick swore that the Sheltie winked at him.

Once in the apartment, Pete sat beside the dining table and followed Rick's movements with his eyes. They were sad eyes, and each time Rick looked at him, he saw his father—and thought of the trust he was placing in his son's hands.

As Rick settled on the sofa and turned his own TV set to the football game and stared, unseeing, at the teams chasing each other up and down the field, his mind was racing. He couldn't afford to move. He'd just bought a car above his pay bracket and he'd have to sacrifice the deposit on the apartment if he left. Chances were slim he could even find another apartment at this price within walking distance of the office—especially one that would permit a dog—and he couldn't afford to pay movers anyway—or a parking fee near his office. Regardless, Rick's mind was working over the list of his friends who were strong enough to lift an end of the sofa he was sitting on and dumb enough to agree to help him move.

Pete was whining now, but softly. Rick looked over at him, in fear that he was building up to another session of howling that would bring Calvin's heavy fist pounding at the apartment door. But Rick saw that Pete was asleep now, his muzzle buried down in his splayed front legs, and Rick couldn't bring himself to try to nudge him into silence. He had lost his master, and he seemed to realize that fully now. He was probably feeling more lost and unsure of what to do now than Rick was.

Rick felt the first warnings of a migraine coming on. He was thinking too hard, he knew—and with too little prospect of finding a way out of this maze. Rick couldn't keep Pete here—at least he couldn't without giving Calvin what he wanted from him. And the very thought of that sent shudders through Rick's body and his temple started to throb. But Rick knew now that he couldn't just toss Pete away either. This would be his ultimate failure as a son. It was one thing for his father to miss the mark continually all these years. It was yet another for his son to do the same—to perpetuate those mistakes down through the

103

generations. Rick had declared long ago that he wouldn't go down the same path as his father had in messed-up relationships.

And there was no question now that Rick had a relationship with Pete. He hadn't had one before he had left for his dad's funeral, but he couldn't deny that he had one now after the man and dog had visited the grave together.

Rick felt the silky softness of hair brush against his hand—and that wet nose again. Pete was no longer asleep. He was in front of Rick now as he sat on the sofa, nudging him and laying his muzzle in Rick's lap. Rick didn't know if it was to assure and comfort him or to seek assurance himself. And he didn't care which it was. Rick's head was clearing and his mind was telling him just to let the decisions slide until tomorrow. The day had already been rough and momentous enough.

Rick flicked off the TV set and rose and padded into the kitchen. Pete followed along beside him and sat in the doorway as Rick filled his food and water bowls and signaled where he was to sleep—on a blanket Rick folded up and laid on the floor under the kitchen window, beside the refrigerator.

Pete watched Rick move from refrigerator to bowl and sink to bowl and to the kitchen window, and when Rick patted the blanket, Pete rose right up and walked over to the blanket and hunched down on it with a huffing sound that Rick took for acceptance and contentment.

Rick switched off the lights in the kitchen and living room and went into the bedroom and beyond to the bathroom, where he showered. He closed the door between his bedroom and the living room, listening for the click that didn't come, the mechanism of the doorknob having become unaligned because of the warping of the door, and climbed into bed and was fast asleep much more quickly than he thought would happen on a day like today.

The next morning Rick awoke with the sensation of being weighted down, to find Pete laying beside him in the bed, his muzzle resting on Rick's side and a foreleg stretched over his hip. Pete was snoring, but quietly. Rick lay there for almost an hour, not daring to move, not wanting to disturb his new companion's sleep—strangely content and whole.

Pete was Rick's dog now. If he had to go, Rick would go too.

* * * *

"I told you about that dog. You were going to get rid of it. You know what the lease says. And you knew it before the dog showed up."

"Oh come on, Calvin. He's been here for nearly two weeks and you didn't even know he was still here. He's a good dog, and he's quiet. He isn't a yap yap dog like the one the guy in 3B has. And you let him stay."

It had been a mistake to say that. And Rick knew it was as soon as the words had come out of his mouth. Pete indeed had been a good dog, smart enough to know that his existence here hinged on that. And Rick knew it had been hard for him. He was a free-range dog; he'd never had to be cooped up in an apartment like he was with Rick. But he had done his part on being quiet for nearly two weeks. Rick had known it was just skirting along the inevitable, though. The one thing the dog and his new master had to do was to get Pete out and to the park a couple of times a day. it wasn't just so he could relieve himself. Pete was an active dog; he had to run free at least a couple of times a day to keep his muscle tone up.

The man and his dog had actually been lucky to be able to spin it out this long before Calvin caught them either coming or going.

Rick knew what Calvin was after, how he would use this for leverage. And Rick had played right into his hands by mentioning the dog in 3B again.

"You know why I let the guy in 3B have his dog," Calvin said. He was wearing a grin on his face. Knowing that Rick had trapped myself. "And the same deal is available to you. You know what I want."

"You can't just play favorites like that, Calvin."

"Well, now, I'll tell you. Between you and the guy in 3B, you would immediately become my favorite."

105

Rick ignored that surged ahead. "I could call the owner of the building and tell him you've let the other dog be here. You might lose your job and your apartment."

"Why, yes you could, Rick. That wouldn't keep you from being tossed out on your kiester, of course—the lease you signed is clear on dogs—but it would give me a good laugh. Bet you don't know that the building is owned by my brother-in-law. He'd overlook anything I was doing as long as I didn't move back in with my sister and him."

The two men stood there, in a standoff, Pete looking up from one to the other, wagging his tail. Trusting in his new master. Rick could see it in his eyes. The nearly two weeks hadn't made any of it easier for Rick. With each passing day, he had grown to love Pete more. Rick hadn't realized how solitary his life had been. Once again he had to wonder if his father had been more attuned to his son's life and loneliness and monotonous routine than even Rick was. With each passing day, Rick increasingly saw Pete as a gift and a life saver.

Calvin broke the silence. "You know what you can do to keep this dog here, Rick. Think about it. But not too long. Tomorrow I call a moving company and as soon as they can book it, they'll be here moving your things out onto the street. Then I won't care where you and your pooch go."

He gave Rick a meaningful look and turned and walked to his doorway. He turned again and said, "I think I'll leave this door open for a while and go back to my bedroom and take a little nap." He winked at Rick then and disappeared into his apartment.

Rick felt himself trembling all over, and he fumbled with his keys and then couldn't quite get the door key into the lock. Pete nuzzled his nose into Rick's hand, and he finally was able to insert the key and turn the lock.

Rick went straight to the kitchen and poured himself a slug of scotch. He chugged that and went back into the living room and collapsed on the sofa. Pete was right there at Rick's knee, raising his paw to his master's leg and looking up at him with those trusting eyes of his.

Rick sat there for perhaps a half hour, Pete in continuous attendance, and then Rick sighed, stood up, and crossed to the door. He locked Pete in and crossed the landing. Rick heard the pawing at his door and Pete's whine—almost like Pete knew what Rick was going to do and was trying to dissuade him. Calvin's door was still open. Rick walked in and slowly crossed Calvin's living space, zigzagging around the exercise equipment that helped keep Calvin so pumped up.

The bedroom door was open too, and when Rick entered, he saw Calvin standing at the window, wearing nothing but a big grin. He gestured toward the bed.

"I changed the sheets just for you," he said.

Rick saw that Calvin was holding two pairs of handcuffs at his side, and he started to back out of the door. But Calvin was quick. Rick turned and was moving fast, but Calvin was faster. He landed on Rick's back and brought him to the floor. Rick continued to try to pull himself along the nubby carpet toward the door, but Calvin was bigger and stronger—much stronger.

"So, you don't want to do it on the bed," he was muttering as he was tearing Rick's shirt, popping buttons with a ripping sound. "We can do it on floor just as well. Or are you having second thoughts? Already starting to pack for that move? Found another place that will take that mutt of yours?"

Rick moaned in defeat. "No, please. I'll do it. Just don't—
"

But Calvin wasn't listening to him now. He'd won—and they both knew he had. He dragged Rick up from the floor like he was a sack of potatoes, but rather than hauling him back into the bedroom, he carried him over to the area he'd marked off as his exercise area and dropped him down on his back on a weight bench where he had a heavy barbell suspended on a rack. Rick made an effort to struggle up to a sitting position, but Calvin backhanded him across the face sharply, and said, "Stay. Either say you're moving or you are going to lay back and take me. I don't like a tease."

Stunned by the unexpected blow, Rick laid back on the bench while Calvin handcuffed his wrists to the suspended barbell at each side and stripped his trousers off.

There was initial pain, Calvin not giving Rick nearly enough time to adjust to him, but once Calvin's cock was buried deep inside him and Calvin was lost in the rhythm of the fuck, thinking only of his pleasure and release, Calvin was much like any

107

other man Rick had been with. It wasn't like Rick hadn't been with men before. And now that Rick had crossed that barrier with Calvin, knowing that this would now become a routine for them, Rick just gritted his teeth, hooked his legs on Calvin's hips, and pushed his mind into an alternate universe—one where he and his dog, Pete, were rambling in a lush parkland.

Later, in the night, Rick heard Pete nudging at his bedroom door until it opened on the misaligned latch. Rick heard the Sheltie padding across the floor and felt the weight of him jumping up on the bed—momentarily disturbing his master with the image of Calvin's weight descending on him in the bed across the landing earlier that day—and Rick lifted his hand and let it fall on Pete's silky neck as the dog nuzzled into Rick's body with a sigh.

There was a full moon out, and Rick had left the curtains open, not wanting to be in complete darkness on this, his first time of giving in to Calvin's blackmail. So, he was able to see the look in Pete's eyes as he lowered his head on his master's belly. It was such a look of trust and contentment that a tear came to Rick's eye and he realized that it was a fair enough bargain, not too much of a price to pay, to have Pete with him.

* * * *

If Mike's Golden Retriever hadn't had the infected paw and been kept for two days at the vets Mike never would have met Rick. More precisely, though, if Mike hadn't been the kind of person he was, their paths would never have crossed.

Mike was just sort of kicking around that day, with little to do, and he decided to go down to the vets and visit Rusty on a whim. Perhaps it was the hangdog look on the face of his other Golden Retriever, Nail, missing his mate and not knowing why she wasn't there that made Mike feel guilty. He had no engagements that day and had planned to just laze around and sun himself on the lawn and maybe take in a movie later. And here, one of his beloved Goldens was locked up in a cage and probably panicked at the thought she'd been abandoned—when she was in pain. For all Mike knew, Rusty could think she'd done something wrong, something to displease him, and was being doubly punished.

So, Mike mentally kicked himself in the butt, pulled his body out of the chaise lounge out on the back lawn, dressed, and headed out to the edge of town where his vet had his office and kennel.

As Mike pulled into the parking lot, which was nearly deserted on a Saturday afternoon, he noticed a car parked over in the corner, near the low-lying branches of a tree, about as far away from the entrance to the vets as it could get.

Parking closer to the entrance, he stepped out of his car and looked over at the other one again. Someone was in the car, in its driver's seat, but hunched over. It was a man, and he seemed to be quaking.

Maybe he's having a seizure, Mike thought. Maybe I should go over and see if he's OK.

This is the sort of person Mike was, and so this is how he first met Rick.

"You OK, guy?" he said when he'd arrived at the car. It was a little Italian sports job and he had to lower his head to peer into the driver's compartment. He could see some sort of rug or fur coat wadded up on the passenger seat when he scanned the compartment. Mike was the cautious type. Finding a man in a car out hiding in a corner of the lot like this raised some "take care" instincts in Mike. He wouldn't have known that was what he was doing when he first peered in the car if he'd been challenged on the issue, but truth be unfurled, he was scanning for some sort of weapon—something the man acting strangely could use on himself or someone else.

The man looked up, a dazed look on his face. Seemingly surprised to see another man staring in at him through the window glass but also numb and slow to react. Mike thought he looked nice and sane enough—in fact he was very good looking and not yet into his thirties. Blond and clean cut, someone who took good care of himself.

But tears were streaming down his face. It didn't take a genius to know that he was in considerable distress. Mike looked him over real well—at least the part of him that he could see from outside of the car, looking for some sign that he was wounded, but not finding anything.

The man was giving him a slightly quizzical look, but he reacted in no other way.

"I said, are you OK, guy? Can I help you . . . do you need . . . could you just roll down your window, please?" Mike made a cranking gesture to help drive home his request.

The man just stared at him for the longest moment, not comprehending, but then it dawned on him that Mike was trying to communicate something to him and was being impeded by the rolled-up window. He leaned over and pressed a button, and the window smoothly retracted down into the door panel.

"What . . .?"

"I asked if you were OK. You seem to be in distress."

"What . . . oh, yes I'm OK. I'll be able to do it . . . soon . . . in a few minutes. Am I . . .?" The man didn't complete the sentence; he just sort of wound down. His head turned from side to side in slow motion as if wondering if he was blocking something in the parking lot, but then he just looked down at his hands in his lap.

"Do what in a few minutes? I don't understand. Is something wrong?"

"No," the man responded, but it wasn't a convincing no; it was a quite possibly yes no.

"Are you alone? Is there someone I can call? Have you been out here for a long time? Are you here to see the vet? Are you on medication? Or is there some medication you should be taking and didn't?"

The man just let the questions pile up, and a confused, and now quite concerned, Mike nonsensically kept adding one query on top of the other, hoping that something would ring a bell with the man, that some question would be one he'd answer and this perplexing—and distressing—mystery could start to unravel.

"Are you here to see the vet?" Mike repeated, having felt that this question had affected the man more than any of the others did.

"Just a few minutes . . . a few more minutes more. Then we'll go in. I think he's asleep, and he isn't whining now. I don't want . . . to disturb him."

"Him? Him who?" Mike asked. But then his eyes picked up the movement in the passenger seat. The rug or whatever it was there was moving. And focusing closer now, Mike could see that it was breathing—if only in belabored fits and starts.

"Is that your dog?" he asked, his voice going soft how, his mind racing ahead, assessing all of the options, close to the answer. An answer he didn't want to be the answer. He didn't know this guy and he didn't know this dog, but Mike worked closely with dogs—and he worshipped the two he had.

Oh, God, he thought silently, don't let this be that.

"I was supposed to bring him in on Thursday," the man said in a low, pained voice. "But I couldn't. I just couldn't. Pete seemed to be getting better. Whenever I checked him out he seemed to be getting better. But this morning I realized that he was only trying to seem to be getting better—for me. I can't . . . I know he's in pain. They told me the pain would only get worse. They told me it was for the best . . . for Pete."

"I'm so sorry," Mike murmured. "I know how hard it is. I've had to . . ." The words caught in his throat. It didn't mean anything to this guy that Mike had had to do it too. Those weren't this guy's dog. It wasn't Mike facing this now.

"I've had him for three years. Got him when my dad died. Dad asked me to take care of him. But I think it was him who was taking care of me. Gave me a life. Made me think of someone else but me."

The guy who hadn't been able to talk before was now gushing it out. The fur ball moved, whined, and a muzzle unfolded and moved over to the guy's lap. Mike could see the eyes now. The dog was looking up into the face of his master now. Trust in those eyes, but also sadness and pain. Mike could see that the dog was trembling. He could tell that the dog was in pain. Tears were still rolling down the guy's cheeks, but Mike could feel his own eyes going misty too. The man snuffled and so did Mike. The dog gave a pitiful little whine, but his gaze up into his master's face was unflagging.

"Sorry, I'm running on," the man said. "Thanks for checking, but we'll do this . . . just a few more minutes."

"How long have you been out here?" Mike knew he should just turn and leave—leave the two alone for whatever last

111

moments they had. But his feet were lead; they wouldn't carry him away from the car.

"Is it still morning?" the man asked.

"No it's getting pretty late into the afternoon." Mike had his answer and he knew now that he couldn't leave. That the man couldn't do it. And he equally knew that it was the right thing to do—for the dog's sake.

"I can walk you in . . . if you're ready," he said.

"A betrayal. I promised my dad I'd take care of Pete."

"Not a betrayal," Mike murmured. "You said you've been with your dog for three years since your dad died. You had him for three years. That's a long time in dog years. Don't think of it as an abandonment. Think of it as a last kindness." And then to take an edge off that, "How old is Pete?"

"Fifteen . . . I think. He wasn't mine; my dad had him for some time before he came to me," the man answered after a long moment of silence.

"Ah, well, then," Mike said. And then they just remained there in tableau, the two men not moving, the dog breathing hard and whimpering—but guardedly, trying to the last to fool his master—to make him think it was getting better. But then, when the pain hit again, begging his master for release.

"It's getting late," Mike said. "They'll close soon. Do you want to come back on Monday?"

"No. No, I can't. I know he's in too much pain. God, I'm such a failure. This one thing my dad ever asked of me . . . and I can't."

"Would you like for me to take Pete in for you? Then it wouldn't be you. I'd stay with him. He wouldn't be alone. I'd make sure they gave his collar to me, and I'd bring it back to you."

"You'd do that for me? For Pete?"

"Yes, of course. I'd hope someone would do it for me . . . if I needed it. But I'll need your name and address or something to take in with me. Is this your regular vet?"

"Yes," the man whispered. "It's our regular vet." He rummaged around in his back pocket and came up a wallet. He extracted a business card from that and handed it to Mike through the open window with such shaking hands that Mike had to chase the vet's card for a couple of seconds before grasping it.

"So, it's OK? You want me to?"

The man didn't answer—he couldn't speak; he couldn't say the words. But he nodded his head. Mike walked around to the passenger side and scooped the Sheltie, Pete, up into his arms as gently as he could, and started walking toward the entrance to the vet. He looked down and saw that the dog was looking up into his eyes now with that trusting, pained look, but mercifully Mike couldn't maintain eye contact for long. His own eyes were full of tears.

After it had started, Mike and Pete's journey to the vet's entrance, though, Mike heard footsteps behind him.

"I can't," the man said as he caught up to them. "I can't let Pete think I've abandoned him at the last."

They went into the consulting room together with the vet and stood there, the man holding the dog's paw and Mike putting a reassuring hand on the man's back to the last. Then the man turned, snuffling, and started, on unsteady feet, to leave the room.

"You'd best not leave right away," Mike said to the retreating back. "Maybe you should sit in the waiting room for a few minutes."

"Yes, maybe you're right," the man said in a low voice as he left the room.

Later, when Mike came out—only briefly stopping in the kennels at the back to hug his own dog, Rusty, and whisper that he'd be back to take her home soon—he offered to take the man for coffee and then to drive him home if the man felt like he couldn't manage it.

The man accepted. The coffee and Mike's gentle way with him calmed the man down considerably.

"My name's Mike," Mike said after he'd brought the cups of coffee out to the sidewalk table.

"Oh, sorry, hi, Mike. I'm Rick. And thank you. I feel much better about it now."

"I'm glad," Mike said, "but it's OK if you don't feel better. I can tell what Pete meant to you."

"I hated that dog. And I hated my dad for foisting him off on me. When he did, as he was dying, I thought it was his last hateful dig at me."

113

Mike didn't respond. He thought Rick was in shock and was overcompensating. He didn't have to see any more evidence than he had that this guy hadn't hated that dog.

Rick, who had been staring down at the surface of the café table when he said that, gave a little nervous laugh and looked up into Mike's eyes, grateful that the man had been sensitive enough not to jump on him for saying that.

"That was just the beginning, just the first couple of days, of course," Rick said. "We actually bonded quickly. But that dog upset my apple cart. He was a ranch dog—he'd spent most of his life on my dad's ranch, herding sheep. That's what Shelties are best for, you know—herding sheep. He'd never been an indoor dog. And here he was, dumped on me with no notice. Me living in a city apartment. An apartment house that didn't allow dogs, and a super from hell. He made my life hell over that dog. I can't even begin to describe what I had to do to keep that dog and me from being tossed out on the street on our tails before my lease was up. It was sheer hell."

Mike said nothing. He just lifted the coffee cup to his lips and took a long, slow sip—providing an excuse for not saying anything.

Rick laughed again. The laugh not as tight this time. No hysterical edge to it. "Best thing that ever happened to me," he muttered. "God, I loved that dog."

Mike grunted—letting Rick know he was listening. Letting him know he wasn't pushing him either way or being judgmental—or, as he almost had mistakenly done at the car, making any of this to be about himself.

"Soon as I got to the end of that lease and out from under that super, Pete and I headed out here, to the edge of town. Got us a little house with a good-sized yard and nice neighbors willing to help with Pete when I had to work long hours or go off on a business trip."

"Good for Pete, that," Mike now said. "Good for a Sheltie to have plenty of room."

"And good for me too," Rick answered, his voice now stronger, more confident. "He was my freedom too—changed my life a lot. In good ways. Best thing that bastard of a father ever did for me. I don't think I gave a shit about anyone but me before Pete came into my life. He taught me to care."

Mike sensed that it was time. "Yep, a guy should always have a dog. I've got two now—Golden Retrievers. A matched set. A dog is good to have. And they say it's always good to get right back on that wagon."

Rick went silent. Mike didn't push further or try to fill in the silence. He could see Rick working that over in his mind.

"I don't know. I don't know how soon . . . or ever."

"Know what you mean," Mike said, "but still . . ."

"A heartbreaker . . . a real heartbreaker . . . when . . ."

"Still. There's heart there. And a lot of good times. Some really good memories that go begging otherwise."

"Yes, I guess, but . . ."

"I saw from your card that we don't live far from each other," Mike said. "Ever take Pete to Penn Park on weekends? They have off-leash days there then. I like to take mine and just let them run. It's good for them. And I enjoy watching all of the dogs myself—seeing the variety and watching them play with each other."

"No. I've heard about the park. But never been there."

"I thought not. Don't remember ever seeing you there. It's a lot of fun. Nice for folks who love dogs."

"Yeah, I bet it would be."

"So, maybe I'll see you there then someday."

"I don't know . . ."

"I'd like that," Mike said. "I'd like to see how you're doing . . . as time goes on." And when Mike said that, he realized that he really did want to see Rick again—and that his interest in Rick didn't really have anything to do with dogs other than having an attraction to any man who cared for a dog as much as Rick had shown he cared for his Pete.

The two sat there drinking their now-cold coffee down to the bottom of the paper cups, both trying to hide from the other that the coffee had been drained a long time ago. Mike felt contented, and he noticed that Rick wasn't shaking any more.

But he also noticed that he was holding Rick's hand in his. He had wanted to be sensitive and supportive, but he hadn't intended to be forward. He had to admit to himself, though, that

115

he was attracted to Rick. He probably wouldn't even have stayed at the side of Rick's car in the parking lot, talking to him, in the first place if he hadn't been. Rick noticed that they were holding hands at the same moment that Mike did. But he didn't withdraw his hand. He looked into Mike's eyes, and what was conveyed between them in that look wrote volumes of what might be possible in other circumstances.

Suddenly flustered, Rick took back his hand and sat back in his chair. He only now realized that both he and Mike had been leaning into each other over the tabletop. "I think I can go back to my car now," Rick said quietly when he had crushed his empty coffee cup and laid it on the table in front of him.

"You'll be OK? Here's my card, by the way . . . in case you'd like to meet up at the park someday and see my Golden Retrievers. And can I have yours."

"Yeah, thanks for the card. And I think so. I think I'll be OK . . . if not today, tomorrow or the day after that. But thanks. Thanks. I don't think I would have been OK if you hadn't come along. That was really kind of you."

"Like I said back there, I would hope that someone would do the same for me . . . if I needed it. And I'm glad I met you." Mike lifted his eyes, hoping that he could catch Rick's eyes with his and repeat just how glad he was they had met, regardless of the circumstance. But Rick was still staring at his crushed coffee cup.

Mike parked the car in the vet's lot when they returned, and he forced himself not to look back as Rick walked over to his car. Mike entered the vet's, glad that he'd gotten back a half hour before they closed up office. He suddenly wanted to see his Rusty again. He wanted to bury his face in her fur and hug her close. And then he wanted to go right home and do the same with Nail.

Later that evening, Mike, already having showered and clad only in a silk lounging robe, heard a knock on his front door.

It was Rick, standing there, hanging his head, and looking like he was about to turn and flee. But when Mike invited him in, he crossed the threshold.

Rick was holding Mike's calling card in his hand like it was a bus ticket and nonsensically said, "Your address was on the card."

"Yes, yes it is," Mike said. "That's what calling cards are for."

"You were telling me about your dogs, your Golden Retrievers, and I thought I might—"

"Ah, yes. Nail's closed up in the back bedroom, but you certainly can—"

Rick started to speak, but then he coughed—and cleared his throat. "You wouldn't happen to have a drink of water I could borrow, do you?"

"I think I can spare one you can have. The kitchen is that way. I'll get you a glass."

They moved into the kitchen like zombies and Mike opened a cupboard and took out a glass while Rick stood at the sink, his hand on the cold water faucet handle, but just resting it there, not turning the water on. Mike came in close behind him and moved the hand holding the glass around to in front of Rick. But Rick didn't take the glass.

"It isn't a drink of water you really want, is it?" Mike asked in a deep, hoarse voice.

"No, it isn't. I don't know what I . . ."

Mike was close enough behind Rick to know he was trembling. And Mike moved even closer in behind him and carefully set the glass down in the sink. Rick's arms were spread away from his body, the heels of his hands dug into the edge of the kitchen counter at each side.

Mike took Rick's wrists in his hands and pressed his body into Rick's back, receiving a shudder as response and knowing that Rick could feel the urgency of him through the thin fabric of the robe and the nearly as thin fabric of Rick's trousers and briefs. Rick sighed and moved his buttocks back into Mike, who then lowered his lips into the hollow of Rick's neck and kissed him. Rick rolled up his buttocks.

The offer—the surrender—was something that couldn't be misinterpreted in the world that both men lived in.

Mike moved his pelvis, raising it and lowering it, his erection sliding up and down between Rick's butt cheeks, leaving no doubt what he'd like from Rick. Rick moaned and turned his face and Mike raised his lips to meet the trembling lips.

But then Mike broke away and moved down the counter, opening a cupboard to keep his hands in check and pulling out a couple of wine glasses. It shouldn't be easy like this, Mike was thinking. Rick was vulnerable and in shock. It would be taking advantage of him to do it like this, here, and now.

"Ummm. I think we both need a drink. White or red."

"What?" Rick was still standing at the sink, quaking.

"Wine. White or red. Go on into the living room and get comfortable. I'll bring out the wine."

Mike wasn't rejecting the idea of sex, but he thought it best to give Rick more time, more room—and an escape, if he wanted it.

"Oh. Uh, red, I guess." Rick turned, and the rapidity with which he fled the kitchen told Mike that he must be having second thoughts. It was good that he had stopped.

But when Mike entered the living room, it was empty. He looked over at the door. It was closed, but that didn't mean that Rick hadn't recovered himself and left the house. But then he looked around and saw that the door to his bedroom was wide open. He always kept that door closed. The dogs had visitation rights in his room, but not free access.

Rick was stretched out on the bed, on his belly, and naked. Mike pulled at the sash of his robe and it fell to the carpet. And then he was on the bed, his body stretched out full length on top of Rick, who was trembling but who murmured an "Oh, god, yes. Please," as Mike began to move his hands and body on Rick's back. Within minutes, Rick dug his knees into the bedspread and raised his hips into Mike's moving pelvis.

"Please. Be good to me. Don't make me wait. Please." Rick was whimpering.

He was ready—more than ready—and Mike slid right into him and they were transported into the rhythm of the fuck almost immediately. Rick was crying and thrusting his hips back hard with each dig of Mike's cock.

"I'm sorry. Am I hurting you?"

"No, no. Please don't stop. Please . . . don't . . . stop."

Rick never did see Nail that evening. That happened the next morning, over breakfast.

* * * *

Mike scanned the edges of the field over to where the three-tiered section of bleachers was positioned next to the little league baseball field. He wasn't there. And he certainly wasn't over to Mike's right where the dog owners had gathered this Saturday morning to sip their coffee and chat while they kept one eye on their dogs cavorting out in the center of the Penn Park field.

It had been two Saturdays since he'd met Rick at the vet's and Rick had come to him at his house. Rick hadn't called him, and Mike didn't think he should push it. He could completely understand if Rick wanted it to be a single encounter. It hadn't been the best of circumstances—most certainly not from Rick's perspective—and Mike hoped that hadn't blotted out his chances altogether. He'd been attracted to Rick. Rick's display of emotion over the loss of his dog might have been a turn off for most guys, but it had been a turn on for Mike. Anyone who could feel that way about his dog was OK with Mike. More than OK.

And he was such a good fuck.

Mike wondered, not for the first time in those two weeks, if Rick was actively gay—or whether he had just been overwhelmed by circumstances. It wasn't usually this hard for Mike to figure out what another guy wanted. But he hadn't been in a relationship since Eddie. And that hadn't ended well. Mike had almost given up hope of finding someone else—someone sensitive and giving. Someone who could feel about his dog the way Rick showed that he felt about his Pete. Someone who could be vulnerable and open up with another man the way Rick had been with him.

Mike just didn't know how to approach this with Rick. Of course, if Rick just didn't show up—as clearly as Mike had tried to extend the invitation to visit the park on Saturday mornings—the opportunity wouldn't even come up.

Mike looked out over the field, searching for and finding, in turn, his Golden Retrievers, Rusty and Nail. Ah, if only life was as simple for him as it was for them.

* * * *

"Peggy, Peggy Collins. Certainly, Mike told me about you—and about your dog. I'm so sorry."

Rick was standing at the door to Mike's neat little house, with the large fenced yard behind it—nearly a twin of his own just eight blocks away. He almost didn't recognize it when he pulled up to the front. He'd been here two weeks previously, of course, but it was dark then and he had been confused. He hadn't even known why he was there—until Mike's body showed him in no uncertain terms why he had sought him out.

He was trying not to show his disappointment. Not because Mike Collins hadn't come to his door. But because Peggy Collins had. Rick thought he had gotten a clear demonstration of how Mike was and what he wanted. But here he was, standing at Mike's door. And there was a Peggy Collins.

He fumbled around, not knowing now whether to hold the boxes out—one of fresh croissants and the other of gourmet dog biscuits—or hide them behind his back.

"I'm sorry. Mike's not here. He's off with the dogs somewhere. But would you like to come in and wait for him?"

She was a nice looking woman. Maybe a little younger than Mike appeared to be—but also a little older than Rick. She had a pleasant smile. They probably were great together. Mike was a lucky guy, Rick thought. So, why did he feel a little deflated with a touch of miserable? It must be Pete. It had been two weeks and he still got weepy over the loss of Pete.

"No, it's fine, I just stopped by to give him these," Rick said, holding the two boxes out to Peggy, who was standing in the door. He was on the second step of the stoop leading up to the square of concrete at the door. He had to hand the boxes up to her. "It's just a gesture of thanks—for what he did for me a couple of weeks ago . . . at the vet's. He went way out of his way for me. Just a box of croissants for you two and some biscuits for the dogs. He told me about the dogs. Two Golden Retrievers. Not anything like he deserves, of course, but I did want to say thanks somehow. No, not the retrievers being what he didn't deserve. The croissants . . . um, sorry."

Rick could kick himself. He was standing there and babbling. Suddenly embarrassed. He hadn't thought it out. He let hope push away common sense. Of course Mike was married and had a regular life. Oh, god, wouldn't it have been awkward if she'd been home or had walked in on them the other night. Mike was that sort of nice guy who certainly would be married. Rick just wasn't thinking straight—hadn't thought straight since he no longer could deny that Pete was sinking fast.

"He'll be pleased," Peggy said, with a smile. "And I'm sure he would tell you that he didn't do anything special, that anyone would offer the help he did. I wouldn't say that about him, of course, but I know that's what he would say."

"Yes, he did say that," Rick answered. "He's really a nice guy."

"Yes, yes, he is. I'll be sure to tell him that you dropped by."

"Thanks," Rick said as he backed down the steps. "And it sure was nice meeting you." He could say it was nice meeting her, Rick was thinking as he retreated to his car—but he couldn't say it was all that nice knowing about her.

The phone rang as Peggy closed the door, thinking that Rick looked like a very nice guy—and then laughing at how many times she'd heard the word "nice" in the last five minutes. Kind of goofy, but in a nice way. She laughed again. Whatever. She liked Rick. She hoped he and Mike would become friends. Then the telephone rang again, insistently. Peggy put the two boxes down on the table next to the door, where they slid toward the wall as she hurried for the telephone in the kitchen and where they promptly disappeared into the space between the table and the wall with a clatter that Peggy couldn't hear from the kitchen.

The telephone call sent her to the hospital to meet one of her girlfriends who had gone into labor prematurely and who wanted someone there for support. Her husband was off in Iraq, she'd lost her first baby by not carrying it full term, and she was scared and panicked. It was a long, but successful delivery, and Peggy was at the hospital into the next day. The trauma of this pushed all thoughts of Rick's visit out of her mind.

When Mike returned home, he found her message and went into his bedroom to change his clothes and call Peggy at the hospital on his cell phone.

When he came back into the living room from a long discussion on the phone with Peggy, he found Rusty and Nail sitting in the middle of the living room, two boxes of messily unwrapped and half-eaten croissants and dog biscuits strewn about them. They had the good sense to give him apologetic stares, and he stared hard back at them and stooped to gather up the debris.

"Now, where did you two find this stuff?" he scolded. "Can't leave you two alone for three minutes."

* * * *

Rick was restless. He needed to snap out of this funk. It had been three weeks and the house was becoming oppressive. He still woke up wondering why Pete wasn't on the bed. He still went to the kitchen door at the usual times, on the point of whistling to Pete to be let out into the fenced backyard, only to realize that there was no Pete. He had slipped into the three-year relationship with Pete, making him so central to his life, without realizing the slice of his life that Pete had taken.

Worse, when he went to the kitchen, his mind wandered back to the one-night stand with Mike, and he shuddered and withdrew from the room.

He'd stopped going out cruising for men at night as he had before Pete had come into his life. He'd given up that scene altogether. Consequently, there hadn't been a man in his life since Pete crept in to fill that gap. Not that they were the same thing, of course. But in time and attention required they were. And in the room they took up in his heart, there was a similarity. Pete had slowly nuzzled his way into Rick's heart and expanded his claim in there to the point that Pete had been more than enough to fill Rick's life. Rick had stopped seeking. Hadn't looked for an alter ego or a close relationship—or even any more one-night stands. Pete had been enough.

But Pete was gone. The void was oppressive. Rick couldn't stay in this house.

And there was the one—the only man in more than a year—who had made such strong and deep and totally satisfying love to him. Rick had forgotten how good sex could be. But it was just the one time.

"I either need a dog or a man," he muttered to himself. And he walked into his bedroom and picked out a pair of tight jeans and his best polo shirt—the one that showed off the musculature of his chest to best advantage. He drew on his black leather boots and practiced his "come hither" smile in the mirror. That made him laugh and then frown. He hadn't thought about doing that for years.

Then he grabbed his car keys and headed for the door. Did he even remember any of the old haunts downtown, he wondered, as he walked to the car. Were any of them still there?

The car stopped sooner than he expected. He'd been daydreaming. He hadn't even driven in the direction of the downtown area. He looked out the window and saw that he was in the parking lot of a park. Several other cars were parked there. That wasn't a surprise; it was a Saturday morning.

Rick got out of the car and stretched. It was dangerous to drive this way, he thought. He'd been zoned out—hadn't even gone in the right direction. He needed fresh air to clear his brain and then he'd take off for the city again. Did he even know where he was? How to get to the city from here?

He was walking through a fringe of woods and found himself at the edge of an open field. A group of people were standing in a semicircle over to the right. They were drinking coffee and chatting.

Rick heard barking and looked out into the center of the field and saw a pack of dogs—several different breeds—running around in circles, playing with each other. While he watched, one of the dogs would break away and run back to the group of people for a reassuring pat and stroke and then scamper back to the center of the field, passing another dog going to check on its owner.

I'm at Penn Park, Rick thought. This is where Mike told me I should come. That I should get another dog and bring him to Penn Park on Saturday mornings. I'm not ready for this, he thought.

Rick turned and started back to the parking lot, which was clearly seen through the fringe of trees, but he heard a bark that arrested his movement. He turned and his heart lurched. A Border Collie was trotting back to the semicircle of owners. Not a Sheltie, but close enough. Close enough to grab at Rick's heart and bring a tear to his eye.

He was still telling himself he wasn't ready for this when he turned and walked toward the bleachers off to the side, by a small baseball field. He couldn't walk over to where the people were standing—he was in no condition to be chatting with people, but maybe he'd sit on the bleachers and watch the dogs play for a while. He sat on the top row, his eyes picking out and following the Border Collie as it returned to the playground and cavorted happily with the other dogs.

Rick's mind was wandering as he watched the swirl of dogs. They were going around and around, with a dog spinning off here and there and then racing back in. Someone had thrown a couple of lengths of knotted rope into the center of the swirl and they were playing tug-o-war with that. Pete was conjured up in Rick's mind spinning out of the melee, although he knew it really was the border collie.

The slam of a car door and a set of new barks made him look over at the parking lot. Mike was standing by the passenger door of a car and opening the back door and letting two sleek, gorgeous Golden Retrievers out. The dogs bounded out into the field, and Mike leaned down and spoke to the driver—his wife, Peggy, Rick saw—and then turned and walked toward the gaggle of people across the field. Peggy drove off in the car.

Rick felt like trying to sink under the bleachers. He felt so embarrassed about the visit to Mike's house. His wife must think he was a nut. And Mike hadn't called in the week since Rick was there. Rick wondered if his thank-you gifts had been seen as petty. They certainly didn't come anywhere near to compensation for what Mike had done for him.

Rick looked toward the parking lot, gauging how he could just sneak off. But Mike had seen him now and was walking toward him.

As Mike got closer, Rick heard him say "Wow" and wondered what that meant?

"Wow?" he asked.

Mike was knocked out by the sexy clothes Rick was wearing—the cruising clothes he had put on, not knowing he was going to be coming to the park. But he didn't admit that that was the source of his "wow." "Oh, I'm just surprised—and pleased— to see that you finally came out. Hi, Rick. It's Rick, isn't it? Glad to see you. Aren't they the limit out there? I could watch those dogs running around happy and free like that for hours."

"Yes, quite a sight . . . Mike. Listen, Mike, about showing up at your house and the croissants . . . I'm sorry, I . . ."

"You came to see me? And those croissants and dog biscuits were from you?"

"Yeah, I'm sorry. Nothing would be enough as a thank-you, but a thought at least . . . and your wife must think I'm a nut. I was still in shock over Pete, I think. I know I sounded like . . ."

"My wife?" Mike said, his voice full of surprise. "I don't have a wife."

"But the woman. The woman at the door—the woman in the car you got out of just now."

"Peggy? You mean Peggy? She's my sister." Mike laughed. "She's been staying with me for a couple of weeks because she had to have her house fumigated. And I'm sorry about not knowing you visited—and not knowing the rolls and biscuits were from you. I'm afraid last Saturday was sort of a panic day. Peggy was called away to be with a friend at the hospital, and your visit must have been swept out of her mind. And the croissants and the biscuits? I'm afraid the ones who got to enjoy those are rambling around out there in the field. Rusty and Nail. They had them all torn apart and half eaten before I even knew they were there. I thought that maybe Peggy had brought them into the house."

"Oh, then that's OK then. Peggy's friend, she isn't . . .?"

"She's fine," Mike said. "A bouncing baby boy. Her husband is being furloughed back from Baghdad to get to see him. But thanks for asking."

Mike was smitten anew. In all of that Rick had picked out that someone was in distress and had asked about that first. Yep, doing what he had done for Rick with Pete was just what Mike could see that Rick would have done for him if the roles were reversed.

Mike looked up into Rick's eyes, and what he saw there gave him hope. And it sent a little charge of electricity through his body.

Mike climbed up on the bleacher and sat on the middle row, not too near but not too far from Rick. He resisted the urge to reach out and touch Rick's hand. Looking for some sort of sign, some assurance that he wasn't misreading what he saw in Rick's eyes.

Rick was looking out toward the field now, toward the dogs.

"You know you really should just jump back up on that wagon," Mike said.

"What? What wagon?" Rick answered. Is he telling me he wants to have me again—that it wasn't just that once?

"You know. Get another dog. I think it would be the dog who would be very lucky."

"You do?" Rick said. He looked at Mike—at the look Mike was giving him. Could it be? he wondered. Is it possible? Is he talking about more than dogs?

"Can you come next Saturday?" Mike asked. I'd really like to see you here next Saturday.

"You would? Well, maybe. Yes, I guess I could come. It's great seeing the dogs. And, yes, seeing them is telling me maybe I should do it. You don't think it would be disrespectful to Pete, though, do you? This soon?"

"No. I think Pete would be pleased. Pleased that you two did so well that you need to fill that hole again."

"Yes, I was just thinking about that earlier," Rick said. "That hole in the heart. That's what Pete left."

They both looked up, hearing the honk of a car horn in the parking lot. Peggy. Peggy Collins. Mike's sister, not his wife. That Peggy Collins.

Mike stood and climbed down from the bleacher—almost reluctantly in Rick's view. "That's Peggy. Tight schedule today and her car's in the shop. Seems like her life has been a series of glitches like this."

"But she's lucky," Rick said. "She has you."

"Yeah, well, she'd do it for me in the same circumstances," Mike said.

"Yep, a very nice man told me that once," Rick said. And then he looked away, not wanting Mike to leave, but not sure where he stood with him, not wanting to reveal his melting want

126

just to be rebuffed. He had the strongest urge to reach out with his hand—to touch Mike's—to try to figure this out. But he resisted the urge, and since he was looking away, he didn't see that Mike, briefly, had held his hand out—wondering the same things, held back by the same fears and lack of surety.

* * * *

"Isn't he a beaut?"

Rick stood there, at the fringe of the park field, still a bit apart from the group of dog owners who had gathered to sip coffee and gossip and watch their dogs dance out in the middle of the Penn Park field on a crisp Saturday morning. He didn't know what to say. A whole range of emotions coursed through his veins.

"Looks like Pete, a young Pete, doesn't he?" Mike said, trying to fill in the gap of Rick's silence. He didn't know whether this was wise or whether it would do the trick—and he hadn't known for sure if he even should be doing what he did nearly nonstop between last Saturday and this. It had been far more difficult and convoluted then he thought it would be. And the circumstances might cause it to backfire. It might be just too pushy.

"Yes, yes, he does." Tears were forming in Rick's eyes. His heart was racing. And there were just too many emotions churning inside and fighting with him at the moment for him to speak.

Mike decided just not to say anything until Rick did.

"Whose . . . whose is he?" Rick asked at last. He couldn't take his eyes off the full-grown Sheltie racing around in the field, first chasing Rusty and being chased by Nail and then the three changing direction, not caring a bit which one was the chaser and which one was the chasee—as long as they were on the move, exercising their muscles like dogs of their breeds and size must do. The Sheltie broke away from the chase and started herding some of the smaller dogs, which were bewildered by the activity but which were amenable to this new game.

Before Mike could respond, Rick laughed. "Do you see him herding?" He asked. "That's the breeding. That's what Pete did."

127

"Yes," Mike said. He took a swig of his coffee. He was happy and relieved. That laugh had brought them across some sort of Rubicon, he thought. This might work after all.

"Whose is he?" Rick repeated.

"Nobody's. At least not now," Mike answered. This was it, he thought. There's no pretending this isn't what it is now.

"Nobody's?" Rick asked, and he turned to look at Mike, giving him a sharp look. "What do you mean?"

"He's on furlough, you could say," Mike answered. "I do this occasionally." (The first lie he had been prompted to give.) "He's in a shelter. His owner died and the shelter is trying to rehome him. They sometimes let me bring the better-behaved ones to the park on Saturdays—to help keep them exercised and alert and happy."

"He looks so much like . . . does he have a name?" Rick was looking at the Sheltie at play again. Mike took this as a good sign. The gantlet had been dropped and Rick hadn't stormed off the field.

And this was it. Showtime.

"Yep. His name's Peteson."

"Peteson," Rick repeated the name. "Peteson, Pete's son." He turned his eyes to Mike again.

"Yes, that's right, Rick. He was sired by Pete. Your Pete. Pretty clever of his owners to play on the name, don't you think?"

Rick met Mike's playful smile with one of his own. They both knew that this was the name Mike had given him. Before he could speak, though, Mike had continued.

"Took me nearly the whole week to find him. I checked with the vet. I knew your Pete was purebred, so I hoped . . . and I was right. Your father was breeding him. I guess you didn't know that. The vet had copies of his papers. The man who had Peteson out there was the breeder your dad went to. He kept Peteson. The man died, though and Peteson there went to the shelter. That part wasn't in my plan. I just thought I'd try to track a puppy that was down the direct line from Pete. But this is first generation. Eight years old. Not a puppy, unfortunately."

They stood there in silence for the longest moment.

"In a shelter now?" Rick murmured at length.

"Yeah, but he's purebred. The people there think he'll be able to find a home. It's a no-kill shelter. Kinda old for placement, though."

Another long pause.

"Pete was twelve when I got him," Rick said.

"Yeah. Older dogs need homes too."

Mike looked down at his side, suddenly aware that he and Rick were holding hands, not knowing who had initiated that. Not caring. Not caring one bit who had made that move.

"I know a café that welcomes dogs—if we sit outside. Not far from here. We'd have to take Peteson with us, though, but I can't see him minding more time out of the kennel," Mike said. "Would you like to go for a cup of Joe?"

"Yes, yes. I'd like that very much."

"Or would you prefer a glass of water at my house?"

"Even better."

KENNEL OPENING

"Wait for it, lad," Graham Morris whispered to Benji, as they both watched the hulking young man being pulled in multiple directions by five Cavalier King Charles spaniels in Graham's direction across a patch of grassland above the Tauranga beach. It was Saturday morning and the bit of parkland adjacent to the New Zealand coastal town's beach was designated as a dog exercise area on Saturday mornings.

Sitting in the shade of an open-sided café between beach and park, Graham knew about the Saturday hours. He also knew that the strapping young man, David Kauea, had a big bunch of spaniels. Graham couldn't have told you they were Cavalier King Charles spaniels, though, or that four of the ones that Kauea had had been New Zealand national champions. But he knew, from research, that Kauea brought them here on Saturdays. Graham was proud of the research he had done since the first time he'd seen the hunky New Zealander.

Beyond that, he knew what Kauea's sexual preferences were, that they complemented his, and that he wanted to try the young man out. Graham was an American, displaced to New Zealand by a frowning family in Baltimore because it was as far away in the world as they could send him. He was content to leave the States and stay in New Zealand because of the checks they regularly sent. He thought the joke was on them, though, because New Zealand's north island was a whole hell of a lot better place to be than Baltimore, Maryland, was in his estimation. And New Zealand men were a lot hunkier.

His eyes slitted as he saw the young man struggle across the parkland in his direction. The five spaniels that were dragging him along—surprisingly good at dragging as small as they were individually and as large as Kauea was—each had a different idea where they wanted to go. The young man's body was magnificent, nearly bursting out of his shorts and T-shirt with bulges of finely formed muscle. Graham wondered how much native Maori was in him. It seemed to be enough to give him bulk and a slightly mean look that belied a gentle temperament until he was lost in want, without making him prone to the big belly that seemed to characterize the more genetically pure Maori.

Benji was a spaniel too. But he was an English spaniel rather than a Cavalier King Charles spaniel. Graham could tell there was a difference, but he didn't really care. He didn't even care whether or not Benji was as pure bred as Kauea's dogs were. A dog was a dog and a spaniel was a spaniel to him, and he was counting on one spaniel being highly interested in meeting another one.

"Now, Benji," Graham said as he leaned down from the seat he was occupying at the fringe of the café and unleashed Benji.

As designed, the English Spaniel was off in a flash. And mere seconds later, Kauea's spaniels no longer were in a disagreement where they wanted to go. As soon as they saw Benji bounding toward them, they all pulled together in that direction. This nearly knocked David Kauea off his feet, despite having feet the size of boats, and he was dragged along toward the café.

Graham made a half-hearted attempt to rise and follow Benji, and he cried out in fake distress, as Benji disappeared in a pile of wriggling dog flesh.

It took David and Graham several minutes to get the dogs separated, during which David was profusely apologizing and expressing the hope that Benji wasn't damaged. Of course he wasn't. The dogs just wanted to do a meet and greet. But Graham did his best rendition of being frightened and concerned for his poor puppy.

"It's not your fault, of course," he said, doing what he could to make his voice sound shaky and unconvinced. He knelt beside Benji and felt the spaniel all over for damage that he'd have no idea what to do about even if he did find any. Benji panted and licked Graham's face, happy for the attention. Graham had a passing thought that he'd like the young Maori hunk to be doing that. "This leash has been giving me the slip. I'll need to get a new one."

"Here, let me check him over." David knelt down beside Graham and laid his hands on Benji. The spaniel liked his touch even better and turned his tongue on the young man. Graham made sure that his hand brushed on David's a couple of times while they both checked Benji over, and he liked the smile that David gave him in return.

"There doesn't seem to be any damage—to your dog at least. You seem a little shaky, though. Can I help you back to your table?"

You certainly can, you big hunk, Graham thought, but he actually answered with a weak, "That would be very kind."

Truth be known, Graham didn't give a shit about Benji. Benji wasn't Graham's dog. He belonged to some bird named Jill, who lived near a bar Graham frequented and who managed to be coming out of her condo building whenever Graham was parking his red sports convertible across the street from her building—and who was too dumb to realize that the club Graham frequented was a gay bar. She obviously liked the look of Graham, though—and Graham was, indeed, very easy on the eyes for his age. She was the first one Graham had thought of when he heard that David Kauea raised spaniels. Graham thought of her because it was a spaniel she was always pretending to walk when Graham was parking on her street.

It was a piece of cake for Graham to get the young David to help him back to his chair in the café—and then to sit with him and to share a cup of coffee. In fact, hooking up with David proved to be very easy indeed. Graham almost regretted that he'd done so much scheming to set up the meeting.

The man was randy, open, and forward, obviously very casual about his sexuality.

In addition to coffee, they also shared a discussion of what brought them to the seaside town of Tauranga on New Zealand's Bay of Plenty, to the south of the main city of the north island, Auckland. David Kauea was born and raised nearby, a good many of his ancestors having been Maori warriors, as indigenous to the island as anyone had ever been. He was an accountant and raised and showed Cavalier King Charles spaniels. He had eight of them.

133

He'd only brought five of them out today. He was gay, a top, liked to fuck casually, and he thought that Graham looked just fine.

Graham, in contrast, was about as foreign to New Zealand as he could be. Banished by his stodgy old-line-Maryland family in the United States for being devil may care about his sexual proclivities, he had washed up on the shores of New Zealand with a pile of cash and a taste in wine. Bored in New Zealand doing little but seducing muscle-bound tops in gyms, he had combined his cash with wine and now owned a winery, Morris Estates, along the coast to the north of Tauranga. His taste in good wine, better wine than he produced, almost—almost—competed with his taste in hunky men to cover and ride him. Neither man seemed to be holding anything back in their discussion.

Tauranga was in the well-established Gisborne wine region, notable for its Chardonnay, Chenin Blanc, Gewürztrammer, and Riesling wines, all of which Graham enjoyed drinking more than he did creating, bottling, and selling. Luckily, he had bought his vineyard lock, stock, vines, bottling room, vintner, and tasting room inclusive and the vineyard operations more or less took care of and paid for themselves.

Just to get it out of the way, Graham voiced a concern: Whereas David was in his late twenties, Graham recently had hit forty. Graham enthusiastically responded that he liked plowing men in Graham's age bracket.

Switching to beer from coffee, the discussions between the two deepened to even more intimate levels than their respective occupations and their mutual love for spaniels and to their deepest, darkest secrets and what they preferred to do in bed. Positions, bareback or condoms, favorite toys, frequency, and where to deposit cum. David proved to be even more devil may care about revealing his sexual proclivities than Graham was. Graham found the sensual openness of the young man both refreshing and highly arousing.

"You look familiar," Graham said, sitting back in his chair and feigning a look of contemplation and scrutiny. "Haven't I seen you somewhere before?"

"Perhaps at Pauli's? I must admit I've seen you there."

"Ah, yes," Graham answered, knowing full well he'd seen the young man at that gay club. "Now I remember. I've seen you with Andrew, one of Pauli's dancers, I believe."

"Yes," David admitted. "Andrew is a sweet fuck. And I believe I've seen you with the construction worker, George. He receives good ratings. I trust he does you well."

"Right," Graham responded.

"I'll bet I could do you better, though," David said, with a twinkle in his eye.

Graham nearly sputtered in his beer. Who was supposed to be seducing who, he wondered. Why the fuck did he think he'd need the dog subterfuge? It took no more than that for the two to square away not only on sexual preference but on sexual role. Andrew, the dancer, was a bottom and George, the construction worker, was a top.

David leaned down and patted Benji. "A fine spaniel you have. I raise and breed spaniels."

"Which is why you have five of them, I suppose," Graham said, using his most attractive smile, and he gave what he hoped was a loving look at the five slobbering spaniels sniffing around Benji with continued interest. Benji was sniffing a couple of them back. Graham assumed these were the bitches.

"I actually have eight."

"Do tell. You must be a very good breeder."

David lowered his face and gave a little smile. Graham chose to imagine that the gesture was meant to move his attention to the young man's basket, where something was straining mightily at the material of his tight shorts.

"My family would have no dogs if they couldn't have spaniels," Graham said in a low voice. It wasn't a lie. Graham's family had had nothing but cats.

Of course, for David Kauea's part, that Graham was a claimed lover of spaniels sealed the deal when push came to shove—although neither found anything in the looks of the other or in a quick and guarded grope that dissuaded either from being interested in the other.

The grope was preceded with Graham rather boldly bringing the conversation to a head by saying, "Yes, I believe you must be a superior breeder. Is it only dogs that you breed?"

And then when David raised his head and gave Graham "that look," Graham continued with, "I admit openly that I would be very interested in your breeding technique." He took David's hand in his and placed it on his crotch. David didn't withdraw the hand. "Would you mind terribly if I touched you too?" Graham asked.

"No," David answered, turning a steely gaze on Graham. "Would you mind terribly if I fucked you? The truth is that George told me you were a really good lay and that you liked to take it hard and deep. I like to give it that way."

Graham melted at how straightforward the New Zealander was.

Agreeing with Graham that Graham's vineyard was probably too far beyond Tauranga to assuage the heat they'd worked themselves into, Kauea took Graham back to the rather large lot but decidedly small house for one man and eight dogs in a suburb of Tauranga overlooking the Bay of Plenty and, bedroom door closed to barking dogs, David fucked Graham to slobbering oblivion just as the American had carefully planned he would do.

As Graham would have guessed, David preferred fucking doggy style, with Graham bent over the bed, resting his weight on his elbows and forearms, while David held his hips in a strong grip with his hands and fucked him in long, hard, deep thrusts. Graham loved it. David seemed to like it enough to do it three times that day before a grinning Graham limped home after delivering a happy Benji back to a not completely happy Jill, confused on why an offer to walk her Benji had spun out to six hours and didn't end with anything more than a "Thanks." Benji was also looking quite pleased with himself, having left three of David's bitches glassy eyed and whimpering.

Graham was around nine weeks later when two of the Cavalier King Charles Spaniel bitches produced pups that weren't fully pure bred. David wasn't wild about that idea, but since he'd happily kept Graham's eyeballs swimming in cum and Graham had been paying most of his bills for those nine weeks, David went with the flow.

The touchiest moment came when David offered Graham one of the puppies. "To remember your poor, lost Benji with," he had said. Graham had had to weave a story of Benji having suffered his demise under a bus a few days after they had initially met.

"I couldn't possibly yet," Graham answered. "It takes me a long time to get over the loss of a pet."

"But the best way is to acquire another one," David said.

"But I have all of your lovely dogs to compensate." Graham nearly choked on that. He'd had David's yapping dogs almost up to the level of the cum David had pumped in him. When the levels met, Graham thought that would be all he could take despite how divinely and forcefully the young Maori cocked him.

This led to another conversation, though. Graham really liked David and being fucked regularly by David, but Graham was getting antsy about being confined to New Zealand's north island.

"I've been thinking of traveling some—in Southeast Asia and maybe even in Europe. I don't want to go alone, though. I'd like you to go with me. I'll pay for everything, of course."

The mention of Southeast Asia caused David to pause. He'd often thought he'd like to travel there if he were free to do so. He had a fetish for small Southeast Asian men—thoroughly enjoying stuffing his big cock in the tight channels of small, brown men to listen to them puffing hard to accommodate him. But he wasn't free. "I couldn't possibly go anywhere for even an overnight. I've told you that's why we have to meet here," David answered. "I've got eight dogs to take care of."

"You could leave them in a kennel."

"There are no good kennels in the Tauranga area. And the cost of kenneling eight dogs would be astronomical."

"I told you I'd pay for everything," Graham said. "And I'd really like for you to travel with me." What he really liked was having David's cock inside him and he'd like to have that while he traveled too.

"Well, as I said, there are no kennels here I'd entrust my dogs to. It's a real failing of this area."

Graham came from a business family. He heard the "Ka-ching" of possibility immediately. "You could open a kennel yourself. Set it up to your liking. Hire someone to do all the shit work and to watch over it while you're traveling."

"It's a thought, but—" David said, obviously giving it a thought.

"I'd partner with you. I'd supply the start-up capital." Graham *really* liked having David's cock inside him.

"Well, it's a thought."

"I know how you could get someone both cheap and reliable. A Thai or a Filipino would be just the ticket. Provide them with work permit employment here, and they'd work like a slave for you and be totally grateful."

"Well . . ." David's imagination went to holding a small Thai or Filipino man under him in a tight embrace while he worked his supersized cock inside a small hole and listened to the impassioned squealing. He hadn't told Graham about this fetish, though.

"I have connections through the international winery association in both countries. I'll be happy to make enquires for you," Graham persisted.

"Well, it's a thought."

"While you're thinking about it, could you fuck me again?"

"Of course."

* * * *

Mr. Crozier called me from the main house and told me he wanted me to come there and see him. I knew what that meant. I was only half way through feeding the dogs and mucking out their cages, so he told me to come when I was done. I could tell he wasn't pleased I couldn't come right away. Neither was I. I was trembling in anticipation. The dogs—six German Shepherds—were restless, though, and when they were like this, I had to be very careful.

They were usually good with me. I handled the guard dogs well, the dogs that guarded the tapioca warehouses at the company plantation near Khon Kaen, upcountry from Bangkok. But sometimes the dogs could sense when I was keyed up, in a hurry to be finished with them. They rarely got human affection and craved it—so they didn't like when I didn't spend as much time with them as usual.

It was nearly dark when I approached the main house. Mr. Crozier lived here alone. He managed the plantation and the warehouses for the company, the only *Farang*—foreigner—here. The other workers were scattered around in huts across the plantation. Only the housekeeper and the cook were allowed in the main house—and me.

Mr. Crozier was like a god in our enclosed little world here. Whatever he told one of the workers to do, they did. The wages were very good for upcountry Thailand, and the local government supported this foreign enterprise in whatever it wanted to do. But like anywhere else in Thailand, there were those who owned and those who were owned. I was one who was owned. Mr. Crozier had told me what my duties were in addition to taking care of the kennels for the guard dogs—and I did what he wanted without question. It was strange and painful at first, but now I wanted it as much as he did.

I moved silently up the ladder to the house. The house was much the same as any Thai house upcountry. Just larger. They were all lifted up on stilts, both because the area flooded and to keep most of the jungle wildlife out of the house. The housekeeper, Lek, lived under the house. She, of course, knew that I visited Mr. Crozier. But neither of us ever mentioned it. I knew what Mr. Crozier sometimes did with Lek too. But neither of us ever mentioned that either.

Mr. Crozier could do whatever he pleased. Over time, it came to please me too.

He was sitting on the side of his bed in the dimming light when I entered his bedroom. He was wearing just a sarong around his waist. His heavily muscled torso always made my breath catch and come in small ragged gasps. He had a dragon tattoo on one side of his chest, the tail of which went up to his shoulder and wound down around his arm. I liked tracing the tail of the dragon when I was lying under him. He was drinking bourbon straight from the bottle, and when he saw me at the door to his bedroom, he leaned over and put the bottle on his nightstand, turned back to me, wiped the back of his hand across his mouth, and motioned to me.

"Come in, Chumphon. Come here. You have made me wait."

139

He had a gruff tone, but I knew he wouldn't beat me as a Thai master displeased with me would do. He would do something else altogether. He was motioning me with his hand to come to him, and I moved across the teak boards on my small bare feet. I too was wearing just a sarong around my waist. But his was raw silk and mine was cheap cotton.

"Sorry, Mr. Crozier," I answered, meekly and with some trepidation. "The dogs were restless and difficult this evening."

"No matter, lad," he said. "You're here now. Waiting just made me harder."

He pulled me into him, between his spread thighs, and embraced me. His mouth was on my belly, kissing it, and the palms of his hands went to my buttocks. He was massaging them as his lips moved around on my belly. I felt the cotton of my sarong drift to the teak flooring as the bare flesh of his hands cupped my buttocks. Kneading them and spreading them. I moaned deeply as the index fingers of both hands found the rim of my anus. He laughed at my little gasp when they entered me.

Then his hands were lifted to my sides and he was pressing me down on my knees between his legs. I unknotted his silk sarong and let it fall to either side. He was hard. Our manager, Mr. Crozier, was aroused—for me. That always made me feel special—and privileged to be able to serve him in this way.

I took his member into my mouth and pleasured him until I felt him raise me with hands on my waist and turn me. As always, I panted, my mouth gaping open and my body shuddering, as he pulled me down into his lap and on his shaft. When he was buried deep inside me, he embraced me closely with his arms, one of his hands encasing and slowly stroking me, and kissed all over my back as he rocked me back and forth. This had brought me great pain at first, but he had taken me this way so often now that my passageway had stretched to fit him. He was big and I was small, but now we were a good fit.

In time, he began to raise and lower me on the shaft with his strong, calloused hand. Faster and faster, pulling me onto him hard, and deeper. He was panting hard and mumbling words I hardly was able to hear through my grunts and groans as he stretched and chafed the shimmering walls of my passageway with his hard, throbbing staff.

I gave him my seed before he released his. And then he continued holding me there as both of us went soft. I knew this was not the last of what he would want from me.

It was during this interlude in which he always told me how much he liked little brown bodies—mine especially. And this time was no exception. But this time he said more and what he said brought me to tears.

". . . and so you must leave the plantation, Chumphon."

"I don't understand, Mr. Crozier. I don't understand why."

"My wife is coming out to join me. I've told you this—that there must be changes."

"But only in where we meet, surely," I answered, trying to keep the sob out of my voice. "I am sorry if I have displeased you. I will—"

"You haven't displeased me, Chumphon. But you cannot be here when my wife arrives. The others will talk. Surely she will learn of you. You understand that, don't you?"

"If you say I must go, then I must go," I answered. But it was with great sadness. I had no idea how I would find a job as good as this one. I already was missing the dogs. And my mother's kitchen had burned down. She expected me to pay for a new one to be built.

"You needn't worry, though, Chumphon. I have arranged a new job for you. In New Zealand. You know where that is, don't you? I'm sure you've always wanted to travel abroad."

I didn't know where it was. It didn't sound like it was any of the nearby villages. Perhaps somewhere nearer to Bangkok, I thought. But I didn't tell Mr. Crozier I had never dreamed of going anywhere but Khon Kaen, and I dared not show any disappointment. It was more than I had a right to expect that he had arranged another job for me. But what kind of job? All I knew of was taking care of dogs.

And, as if he had read my mind, he answered that. "You will still be working with dogs. You will be helping to run a kennel of dogs. You will just be doing it in a whole new world."

I couldn't even fathom at the time what he meant about a whole new world. But he certainly was right about that.

141

And I no longer was giving this much thought. I felt him coming alive inside me again, and he turned me and pushed me up onto his bed on my back and was kneeling between my thighs. I arched my back and reached my arms out to grab fistfuls of his rough-texture bedspread and to sigh and moan as he began to rhythmically thrust himself inside me once more. One of my hands went to his chest and traced the dragon's tail down his arm—for the last time.

One last time, as he already had a plane ticket for me to leave the next day.

* * * *

Chumphon had been at the Kauea Kennels for nearly three weeks before he observed something that made his heart race. His new job was great even though this island wasn't anything like the Thailand upcountry he came from. He had little trouble with the language, as Mr. Crozier had made him improve the English he'd taken in school. Mr. Crozier certainly wasn't going to bother to learn Thai. But otherwise Chumphon felt completely out of place. The terrain was so different—not that he'd traveled enough to feel this was an island. He'd been to the beaches of Phataya, and the beach at Tauranga was much the same even if the buildings and foliage were different.

But the people were very much different. All of them *Farangs*, like Mr. Crozier, if friendlier and less demanding than Mr. Crozier. But Chumphon guessed he was the *Farang* here, not them.

Mr. Kauea was overwhelming, although he certainly was friendly. He was even bigger than Mr. Crozier was and not quite the *Farang* that Mr. Crozier was—or that his older friend, Mr. Morris was. But he was different in a disturbing way. Not exactly disturbing. More the same feelings that came over Chumphon when Mr. Crozier called Chumphon to his house. Mr. Kauea didn't talk to Chumphon the same way he talked to other people when they were around. And there was something in that like how Mr. Crozier had talked differently to Chumphon than he did to other workers on the tapioca plantation. And Mr. Kauea touched

142

Chumphon when he was talking to him—just like Mr. Crozier had.

Mr. Kauea was a little darker than the other *Farangs* here. And of larger stature. Something that seemed closer to New Zealand's own sense of wildness and primitive instincts. Something more of the island's history than people like Mr. Morris was, who spoke almost an entirely different language than Mr. Kauea did, even though they were both speaking a form of English and seemed readily able to understand each other—well, most of the time, and certainly better than Chumphon, with his rudimentary English, could understand either one of them.

When Chumphon could take his mind—and, often, his fantasies—away from Mr. Kauea, they turned to what occupied most of his days and evenings—the dogs. In these terms, Chumphon could only say he was delighted in the change in his life. He had loved his German Shepherds, but they had been trained to be guard dogs and thus were something to carefully fear and respect as well as to love. The spaniels Mr. Kauea owned, on the other hand, were bundles of happiness and slobbering love. There were other dogs at the kennel from time to time, owned by other people in the region who were leaving them while they traveled, but it was Mr. Kauea's spaniels alone that made Chumphon's new life a delight.

The only downside to this life was that Chumphon missed the attention that Mr. Crozier had given him—more than he ever imagined he would. Mr. Crozier hadn't courted him in any way. He had just told Chumphon what he wanted when Chumphon came to work on the tapioca plantation. Few Thai living upcountry had a choice in where or whether they would work. It was a privilege just to have work. Mr. Crozier had just taken from Chumphon what he wanted. Chumphon had wondered about this, but Lek had told him that Mr. Crozier had done the same with her—that all *Farangs* in the upcountry just took what they wanted from Thai people, and that this was the way of the upcountry. Chumphon had not even thought of objecting or resisting. And now Chumphon was surprised at how much he'd come to want it.

Which brought his mind back to the hulking Mr. Kauea he now worked for.

Chumphon had little expectation that he could receive the same attention from Mr. Kauea that he had from Mr. Crozier until that day he went to the house at the kennel to report that one of the spaniels seemed to be limping. As he passed the side of the house, he heard noises from inside and spied them through the open window. The older man, Mr. Morris, was leaning over a bed on his elbows and Mr. Kauea was fucking Mr. Morris from behind—like a dog, like the muscular, overpowering German Shepherds Chumphon had seen breeding at the kennel in Thailand. Both men were naked.

Both were large-boned as Mr. Crozier had been and were not as sun-kissed dark skinned on their upper thighs and groins as they were elsewhere. Chumphon had found this strange and intriguing—and, yes, a bit arousing. Thai people were dark all over. They didn't have their manhood and their buttocks emphasized by whiter skin around it.

The young Thai stood, mesmerized, by the size and power of the New Zealander and by the sounds of pained passion coming from the older man, as he bent over the bed, legs spread, fists digging into the bedding, and tongue hanging out on a face with eyes glazed over in ecstasy.

Mr. Kauea was the largest-built man down there Chumphon had ever seen, and it seemed impossible that Mr. Morris could take it all as it repeatedly withdrew and then thrust back inside, sending Mr. Morris' body to shuddering and jerking. But take it Mr. Morris did. And from the older man's reactions while he was taking it, Chumphon decided that he wanted it too. The thought of his own slight body taking it frightened Chumphon. He remembered how long it had taken him to sheath Mr. Crozier's staff without constant pain fighting with the pleasure, and Mr. Kauea was much larger than Mr. Crozier. But still Chumphon wanted it. And he had adjusted to the size of Mr. Crozier. In time he could adjust to the size of Mr. Kauea too, he was confident.

That evening, he came to Mr. Kauea as he had come to Mr. Crozier, silently, on bare feet, and only with a cotton sarong wrapped around his waist.

Mr. Kauea was sitting on the side of his bed, dressed only in sleeping shorts. His body was magnificent, muscular, bronze-skinned, and with primitive native tattooing that made Chumphon's heart race with the image of coming to him to perform some primordial rite.

The massive New Zealander looked up to see Chumphon standing in the doorway in the dim light. If he was surprised, he showed no evidence of it. Indeed, he reacted as if their coupling was inevitable. Later, when they spoke of what they had done, how Mr. Kauea had used Chumphon's body repeatedly, Mr. Kauea had said that if Chumphon had not come to him, he would have come for Chumphon. He had asked Chumphon if that would have made the young Thai angry or unwilling, Chumphon had not been able to understand what he was asking. Mr. Kauea was his employer; Chumphon would given him anything he wanted.

As he had stood in the door, neither man spoke, but heavy breathing could be heard from both sides of the room. Chumphon worried the knot of the sarong at his waist and it fell to the floor in folds. His erection told David all he would need to know of Chumphon's want and intention. His berry-brown body was perfectly formed, paling in size, though, to that of the New Zealander. David's breath came even heavier as he thought of the massiveness of his cock working the passageway of such a small, perfectly formed man. It was his fetish. A man couldn't do anything about the fetishes he had.

The New Zealander lifted his hips off the surface of the bed enough to slide his sleeping shorts off.

It was Chumphon's turn to gasp and take great gulps of air—Chumphon's turn for his channel to twitch at the expectation of that big, erect club possessing him fully. If anything, it was more massive than Chumphon had believed it to be when it was poking Mr. Morris' hole. He began to tremble and to moan softly.

David extended a hand and said the only words expressed in the room for the next hour. "Come to me, if you will. Don't, if you are afraid. It is your choice. It may not be possible, but I want to try. If it's not possible, though, I'm not sure you can remain here. The temptation is too much."

Chumphon was very much afraid. Mr. Crozier would not have given him a choice; he would have just made Chumphon take it. And from what Mr. Kauea was saying, it wasn't really a choice here either. He would lose his job. But in this case, Chumphon himself wanted it too much for there to be but one choice. This new world Chumphon had moved into was so much more arousing than Thailand and the tapioca plantation had been.

The young Thai cried out in pain and ecstasy as he bent over the bed and Mr. Kauea covered him from behind and slowly worked his thick, long cock inside Chumphon's slowly yielding channel. Mr. Crozier had opened him up, but there was so much more work to be done to accommodate Mr. Kauea.

There was a time when each believed Chumphon's passage just could not accommodate the size of the cock, but both worked hard at it with grunts and groans, both wanting it. And then, miracle of miracles, Chumphon felt his passage relaxing and stretching, and the shaft was sliding up inside him. He cried out so loudly in the effort that howls went up from the kennels behind the house. Neither of the men cared. The music of the dogs lent atmosphere to the primordial rite of taking and receiving. Being primitively fucked like a dog, as, fully saddled, David started his plowing in earnest.

The fuck became wild, David thrusting hard, deep, rapidly, but daring not to pull more than half way out of the channel for fear it would close again. But the young Thai wanted the deep possession, a connection he had never experienced with Mr. Crozier. At the height of passion, Davie buried a fist in Chumphon's thick, black hair and arched the young man's back, pulling his head up to David's bulging pecs, as he thrust, thrust, thrust.

Chumphon came with a great cry, and the rhythm of the fuck changed, became slower, slid deeper, withdrew further before gliding back in. Chumphon's passage had been reamed to David's specifications and he would never have the trouble saddling the young Thai again that he had initially. Three further takings that night would establish the fit forever.

David wrapped an arm around Chumphon's waist and rose up, away from the bed. The exhausted, but moaning and sighing body of Chumphon hung limply, bent over, buttocks nestled into David's groin, feet off the floor and arms and legs dangling in front of him, as the strong, virile New Zealander continued to fuck him in long slides until, with a weak yip sound Chumphon came again, his cum dribbling down his thighs.

Only then, with a great Maori warrior cry, did Kauea release his seed in three prodigious bursts, the cry setting the dogs in the kennel to howling once more.

Chumphon slept in David's bed that night and every night afterward, fully content in this new life of his, growing accustomed to the gentle touch of the young Maori's fingers in the night that coaxed Chumphon to rise on all fours to be fucked again like a dog. Chumphon never once thought of denying the other man's pleasure—his pleasure as well.

* * * *

"Well, hello, who is that?" Graham asked as he unfolded himself from his special production Zetini Haast Barchetta sports car as David stepped down from the front porch of his house. Down the hill, by the corner of the kennels, a young man was loading two sleek Airedales into a Land Rover.

"I wondered when you'd discover Clark," David said, as he walked over to the red sports car. "I'm surprised you haven't run across him at Pauli's. I think you'd find him . . . invigorating. He's every bit as good as George is."

Graham turned and gave David a sharp look. "That's what I find so unique about you," he said. "There isn't a jealous bone in your body." It also, he didn't want to reveal, was one of the aspects to David Kauea he found to be maddening. He wanted a man to care enough for him to be jealous. "You wouldn't care if I walked down there and he fucked me on the hood of his Land Rover, would you?"

"Not if it was what the two of you wanted to do. I don't waste time on sexual games and petty jealousies," David said. "I take the gifts that life brings me gladly and don't resent others doing likewise. You don't think you are the only man I'm fucking, do you?"

He was looking downhill and Graham followed his line of sight. The young Thai kennel helper Graham had tracked down for David had four of the short-term dogs on leashes and was taking them for a walk. The older American felt a surge of jealously. But he was careful not to say the first response that came to his mind—or any response, for that matter. He didn't want what he was getting from David to stop. But he did let the matter seethe in his mind.

So that's how it is, he thought. I was afraid of that. David is fucking the cute little Thai piece I bought for him. I should have known better. I don't remember there being any female kennel workers available, though.

"Would you like me to arrange a hook-up with Clark?" David continued in a calm voice as if he had no idea what Graham was thinking—or that he didn't care. "I think he would enjoy you as much as you would enjoy him. In fact, I can hardly wait to enjoy you again myself."

"No thank you. I'm a one man at a time type man," Graham answered, not being able to resist any longer. He had answered this way on purpose—as both a challenge and an admonition, but if David caught the challenge, he didn't reveal it, or rise to it. David was such a simple, open sort of guy. He made Graham feel like a schemer and just a bit dirty, which is not a feeling Graham wanted to indulge in. If the young man wasn't such a sexy lug and didn't have such a big cock and know exactly what to do with it, Graham would be off and running in finding someone else. He seriously thought he was getting too old to be competing with the likes of the little Thai trick being pulled along by those dogs down in the meadow.

He did, though, like the sound of David saying he couldn't wait to enjoy him again—and that was another thing Graham observed about David: that it appeared that he wouldn't hold back with Graham in sex just because he was spiking someone else too. From that perspective, Graham was forced to accept that David's willingness for him to pursue the Clark man with the Airedales was an open, honest response.

It proved true that David both didn't want to wait for what Graham had driven into Tauranga in his fancy locally produced sports car to get and that he wouldn't stint in fucking Graham even if he also was doing the kennel helper. They only made it as far as the dining room, before David had Graham bent over the table and was fucking him in the doggy style that they both enjoyed so much.

Afterward, while they were sitting on the porch, drinking beer; discussing a bit of business, since they were co-owners of the kennel; and watching Chumphon pad around the kennel down the hill, Graham broached the subject he'd been building up to for weeks now.

"How is the Thai helper, Chumphon, working out?"

"He's doing well in the kennel."

And even better in the house lying under you, Graham thought. But he didn't go there even if he couldn't get it out of his mind. "Well enough to be left with the kennel for a couple of weeks?"

"Well, I don't know . . ."

"You know I tracked him down and arranged to bring him over so that you'd be free to travel. I have brochures on Paris and London in the car. I'm getting antsy on this small island. And I don't want to travel or to sleep alone."

"The island's not that small," David answered. "And I don't really think I can get away now—not for some time."

I understand perfectly, Graham thought, slightly bitterly, since this was his doing—not that he had meant it to turn out this way. David didn't want to leave because he didn't want to be away from Chumphon for any length of time. Chumphon had just proved to be too tasty a morsel for David to resist. At some point in their relationship, David had revealed to Graham his weakness for small Southeast Asian men. The revelation had come too late to prevent Chumphon's arrival, unfortunately. And then, of course, he had to be such a beautifully formed little man.

What was it David had said? That he just went with the flow of life and took what came his way as a gift? Graham was getting old. Maybe he was manipulating life too much. But then, maybe not.

"Where did you say that Clark guy exercised his Airedales? They look too athletic to be house or lap dogs."

"I didn't say," David said in a somewhat distracted voice. He still had his attention locked on Chumphon giving attention to the dogs in their cages.

"But do you know?"

"Yes, I believe he likes to walk them in the Papamoa Dune Wilderness Area on Saturdays."

The following Saturday morning, Graham was sitting on a bench in said wilderness area, as he and the Airedale puppy Graham had taken on a trial basis from a pet supplier watched Clark Stringer, the owner of a men's gym and quite obviously one of the gym's best customers, walking toward them on a pathway with his two Airedales on a leash.

Graham leaned down and whispered, "Oh look, girl, there are two very fit male Airedales bearing down on us with their tongues hanging out. Just let me slip your leash here and go do what comes naturally."

As he unsnapped the leash, he had a nanosecond of second thought, but he had taken David's view of life to heart. There was no reason he had to give up the Maori hunk completely, but there also was no reason there wasn't room in his sex life for a bodybuilder hunk named Clark either.

OBLIVION

"And I don't believe there's any place like Bar Harbor in the late summer. There's a beach just below my family cottage there where some of the hottest men come that time of the year. You'd fit in very well there. So, we really must . . ."

Tim was looking out on the street from where he and Howard were sitting at the sidewalk café on Wisconsin Avenue. There was a man across the busy-traffic street, in front of the Bethesda Residence Inn, who was walking two Cavalier King spaniels. Slender figure, but broad shoulders—the man, that was, not the dogs. Straight as a ramrod. Tim bet the man kept his body in great shape and was doing well with the battle against time. Expensive-looking suit. He looked almost European. Gray sideburns but his hair still auburn on top—and every hair in place. He reeked of money—and of exquisite taste, given the choice in dogs. Tim liked pedigreed dogs. He liked pedigreed men too—and older. Not too old to cock well, but a bit past forty at least.

Tim imagined the man stripped down to a Speedo and playing with his dogs in the surf on a beach—somewhere up north, Maine maybe. But while it was still warm enough to swim in the ocean. He liked the cut of the man, slender at the waist, but a well-muscled chest and biceps—at least that's how Tim imagined him. Hair on the chest, but in an intriguing cascade down from underneath both pecs, down a flat belly, and curling into the low-rise waistband of the blue Speedo. Salt and pepper hair. A nice bulge at the basket and good, strong, firm legs. Tim bet the man ran regularly.

* * * *

The beach was one of those exclusive places that rich residents of weathered wood-shingled, rambling mansions they called their weekend cottages banded together to keep for the use of a small tight community that only appeared from the city three or four times a year. The houses lined a bluff well above the sandy beach, and if you stretched your towel out where Tim envisioned he had, you could be in the sun but away from the prying eyes on the decks of the houses above. It was a place where there was hardly any beach traffic during the week—mainly the servants in the houses above with nothing to do for weeks on end until receiving notice that the masters of the house would be there. Tim only thought of the male servants. The women would be busy actually doing something—too busy to come down to the beach. These were mainly chauffeurs and gardeners and handymen—hot young men who shared the secret of cushy, nondemanding jobs with their sugar daddies. They were mostly what could be seen on this beach during the week. And then young men like Tim who had heard of the hot men on this private beach and sneaked in for some action of their own.

Tim is lying on his towel, his attention split between the elegant older man playing with his Cavalier King spaniels in the surf and two young men up the beach, who have laid out one large towel and are already stretched along each other's bodies, facing each other, and kissing and touching. Other than these men, the beach is deserted. And such a beautiful, sunny, warm day. It is a wasted week day—well, for everyone but Tim and these other guys on the beach. No doubt the beautiful weather wouldn't hold into the weekend when at least a few of the "cottages" above would be occupied.

Tim has taken off his own bathing suit, seeking that all-over tan. He's turned toward the ocean, sitting, with legs spread and forearms on raised knees. The older man in the surf turns and looks at him and then up the beach at the couple, where Speedos have already been shucked and the two are turned to each other on their sides, the hands of both of them busy between their bodies, their lips plastered to each other.

The man smiles and starts to walk toward Tim. Tim spreads his legs further and reaches down and cups his balls and cock with a hand, giving the man a sultry smile. The man stops on the beach at the line where the surf reaches its highest, a line changing from the dark tan of wet sand to the dry, white sand of the upper beach, a line demarcated by a band of small, mostly broken up sea shells. There, in that spot, the man slowly strips off his Speedo, and Tim swallows hard and moans at the sight of how beautiful the man's body is and how well-equipped he is. All power and grace, aged extremely well. As the man stands there, Tim goes to half erection, lifting it in his cupped hand as it lengthens and thickens so the man at the tide's edge gets a good view of Tim's arousal. Then he arches his torso back and spreads his legs wider and gives the man a saucy little look.

The Cavalier King spaniels are bounding happily around the man as he starts to walk again, slowly, but deliberately, toward Tim. As the man reaches Tim, he kneels on the towel between Tim's spread legs and buries his fists in the sand at each side of Tim's chest. They hold there momentarily, staring into each other's eyes, conveying just what each wants. Then the man dips his face down to Tim's and Tim opens his lips for the kiss and sighs at the sweet taste of the man's mouth.

After a sweet kiss, the man's face moves further down and his mouth closes over Tim's cock. Tim sighs and closes his eyes.

The spaniels lay down at each side of the blanket and start panting happily. Tim hears the panting but takes a few moments to realize that it isn't just the spaniels. He is panting as well. The man's face is back, pressing into Tim's, and his tongue invades Tim's mouth and moves in and out, deeper into the cavity with each renewed invasion. More insistent, more brutal, more possessing. Fucking Tim's mouth cavity with his tongue. Tim gags and is finding it hard to breathe, but he doesn't want the man to stop. He opens his mouth as wide as he can, wanting the man to climb inside and take him completely.

One of the man's hands is wrapped around Tim's cock and is squeezing and stroking it. Tim moans and moves his hands around to the man's back, palming his shoulder blades and pulling the man's torso down to his chest, seeking to merge their bodies, make them one. The man's now fully erect and very proud cock is rubbing up and down on Tim's belly and is dueling with Tim's own cock. He traps both cocks with a hand and strokes them together.

No lover like an experienced lover, Tim thinks as he jerks and ejaculates for the first time. And only an experienced lover knows that there is more to come, if properly coaxed.

The man pulls away from fucking Tim's mouth with his tongue and his mouth moves down to the hollow of Tim's neck, where his tongue traces the throbbing vein there. Tim looks over toward the other men on the beach to see that one is on his belly on the towel and the other has mounted him, straddling his hips between his legs. His hands are on the other man's shoulder blades and his bulbous buttocks are flexing and releasing and moving languidly back and forth between the other man's butt cheeks.

Tim's own man has moved his lips to Tim's nipples, but his dick is still stroking Tim's belly.

Tim moans and whispers something, and the man whispers back. Tim reaches over into the beach bag beside the blanket. One of the spaniels leans his muzzle over to Tim's hand, and he licks the tip of Tim's finger. Tim smiles and pets the spaniel on the muzzle but then he jerks a bit and arches his back and lets out a moan. The spaniel has turned his muzzle away. There is another tongue giving Tim attention, though. The man has moved down and wrapped his strong arms around Tim's thighs and parted and lifted them and his tongue is invading Tim's ass channel.

Tim turns his head to guide his hand into his beach bag in search of the condoms and lubricant he has placed there. The young men down the beach are going at it hot and heavy now, the dominating man having brought the other up on his knees and wrapped his arms around the other's chest. The bottom has arched his back into the chest of the top and reached back and cupped the back of the head of his assaulter. The top is banging the bottom hard in loud, slapping sounds that reach their way to Tim on the sea breeze along with the cries of the young man being deep fucked.

The cries of passion are becoming louder, more distinct, and in stereo. It takes Tim a moment to realize that some of those cries are his, as the man is crouched over his chest again, his cock head has gained entry inside Tim's channel, and his hard tool is beginning to thrust deeper, harder, deeper, harder, deeper . . .

* * * *

". . . and the yacht's just up in Baltimore. We could take the sea route to Bar Harbor. I've just had the vessel refurbished. I think you'd really like what I've done with the captain's cabin. There are mirrors—even over the bed, and . . ."

"Uh huh, nice," Tim murmured. He could feel the toes of Howard's socked foot nudging up under the hem of his trousers and rubbing against his shin.

Tim had first met Howard at the law firm where Tim, still in law school, was clerking. Howard apparently was some sort of important client—at least everyone had been told to hup to on that day when Howard came in. There were more senior partners sitting at hopeful attention in the conference room that day than Tim had ever seen there before.

They had been at it—all with their coats off and looking like they were in a disaster-relief planning session, all except for Howard Crandal, who sat there in his expensive three-piece suit, cut to his brawny, Zeus-like body, and perfectly groomed gray hair and manicured nails on his beefy, gold-banded fingers, looking all tanned and relaxed. The disaster relief image had come to Tim's mind because that's what he'd heard one senior partner tell another that they would have to do around here if they lost the Crandal account.

Tim had been called from the file room with some files they needed in the conference room. As he walked across the floor to the head of the table, where the managing partner was sitting, Tim felt Howard Crandal's eyes follow him. He thought he recognized that look.

He became sure he had correctly assessed the look Crandal had given him in the law firm's conference room more than a week later when Tim next saw Crandal.

Law school was expensive and Tim had expensive habits. It was a good thing he was a looker and had a great body too, because he was using that in a second job to make ends meet.

Tim was a dancer in the Green Lantern, a gay bar off Wisconsin Avenue, on the outskirts of the town of Bethesda that had been swallowed by the creeping tentacles of the greater

Washington, D.C., metropolitan area. Tim danced a pole in a G-string on a small stage there for three sets a night, two nights a week. He also, if everything seemed right, would let a patron fuck him in one of the cubicles behind the stage between sets. He made more money these two nights than he did from his part-time job at the law firm. It all helped to keep him in law school—and, he thought, was better than what most of the other students were doing to stay in school. And he didn't have parents who would subsidize him.

One of the other dancers asked him one night how he could do this, considering what he wanted to do in life and, in particular, how he could let some of the older guys who came to the club fuck him. Tim thought on that for days before tracking the other dancer down and telling him that, first, he liked older guys fucking him. But, beyond that, if they were slobs and for those times he was dancing the pole and guys were wolf whistling and making suggestions and touching him wherever they could reach before a bouncer intervened, Tim just turned his mind off and thought of being someplace else and doing something else. He just drifted off into oblivion. The other dancer just gave Tim a funny look, no doubt having forgotten he even asked. But Tim was studying for the law. He liked to pin things down—when he wasn't daydreaming, of course.

Howard Crandal and he had encountered each other for the second time because Crandal had come into the Green Lantern while Tim was doing one of his stints on the pole. They didn't do more than make eye contact and both do a double take at seeing each other in this venue, but at that instant, Tim remembered the look Crandal had given him while he walked the carpet alongside the conference table back at the law firm, and Tim knew what Crandal was and what he wanted.

So, when Tim went back to the dressing room at the end of his last set, he wasn't at all surprised to see the message sent backstage to him—in pen on a bar napkin—proposing that Tim go have a coffee with Crandal at the outdoor café across the street from the Bethesda Residence Inn the next afternoon at 3:00 p.m. Crandal was definitely in Tim's zone of good-looking, well-built, rich old guys, so he'd shown up as scheduled.

It wasn't a real good venue for Tim. He had a hard time focusing when there was a lot going on around him, and Wisconsin Avenue in Bethesda in the midafternoon was one very busy place.

He smiled at Crandal, who smiled back at him and augmented the toe rubbing on Tim's calf with a hand dropped to Tim's thigh.

"The bed I had put into the owner's cabin is king sized and it has a vibrator. Those aren't as popular as they once were. I can't really understand why . . ."

"Um humm," Tim murmured. The man walking his Cavalier King spaniels across the street had moved on now, but Tim felt someone watching their table, and when he looked back toward the door into the café's interior space he saw that there was a young, handsome guy about his own age, looking intently at Howard and him from just the next table and taking in everything Crandal was talking about with a funny, intense look on his face.

But there, beyond that guy, Tim's eyes focused on the host at the reservations table just outside the door into the café. He was maybe in his late forties. Tall, well-muscled. Sort of a Greek look about him. And dressed in some sort of uniform.

" . . . has a full crew, so we wouldn't even have to come up for air before we'd passed Long Island," Crandal was saying.

"Yes, interesting," Tim offered.

* * * *

They had exchanged looks even as Tim was walking up the gangplank onto the cruise ship he was taking out of Baltimore Harbor for a long weekend cruise to Bermuda. The officers of the crew were standing in a long line of pristine-white uniforms on the rail three decks above the gangplank. The one with the most gold braiding on his uniform caught Tim's eye, and they exchanged interested glances in a way that Tim had learned to recognize oh so well.

Even then it was a surprise to Tim when he received the invitation to sit at the Captain's Table on the first night out to sea. The captain turned out to be that man who had been wearing the most gold braiding on his uniform that afternoon while the passengers were embarking.

The captain was tall and well-built. He was maybe in his late forties and had the look of a Greek god about him, a mature one, though, a regular Zeus. He certainly was in full command on this ship. The rest of the crew seemed to scuttle around doing his bidding without him even having to give a verbal command.

Tim is sitting beside him at the table, obviously a place of honor, and the other passengers at the table are looking speculatively at Tim, wondering what manufacturing mogul he's the son of. Tim feels the socked toe work itself under the hem of his trousers and move up and rub against his shin. When Tim feels a strong hand squeezing his thigh, he turns his face toward the captain, who is giving him a piercing look.

"After dinner I will show you the captain's cabin and we will fuck." It is whispered in Tim's ear, but it isn't a request. Tim knows it's a command. Two of the captain's officers are standing near the captain's table and giving Tim a look that tells him in no uncertain terms that out here on the open seas the captain will have what he wants.

Tim stops inside the door into the captain's cabin and is caught short, standing there in awe. Facing him is the foot of a gigantic four-poster bed, set in an alcove. What catches his attention, though are the mirrors—on the walls on each side wall of the alcove, on the back wall, and even on the ceiling above the bed.

He shudders and leans back into the captain, who is standing close in behind him, kissing him in the hollow of his neck, his arms wrapped around Tim, and his hands working the buttons on Tim's shirt and then the buckle and zipper of his trousers. And then his cock. Holding Tim there and stroking his cock, both of them watching in the mirrors, until Tim ejaculates.

The captain is standing over Tim, the gold braid once cascading down the front and sides of his pristine-white jacket now binding Tim's wrists to the headboard above Tim's head and his ankles high up on the posters at the bottom of the bed. The captain is naked from the waist down, a gigantic erect phallus curving up from his belly. He's still wearing his jacket, but it is open in front, revealing a deep, strong-muscled chest.

The captain is asking how Tim likes his chest. Has he ever seen such a barrel chest, the captain asks. He says it's because he is a champion swimmer, that it has given him the breath power and stamina to go for hours. He says Tim will like that, and he laughs and Tim cries out as the captain's cock breaches Tim's channel ring, and the captain starts to breath in and out and stroke in and out, in and out, in long, deep, rhythmic strokes, making Tim imagine he is in a scull listening to the rhythmic cadence of the strokeman's call.

The world is in motion, and it takes Tim several moments to realize that they haven't hit rough seas but that the bed itself is vibrating. The captain is grinning down at him and stroking to the rhythm of the vibrating bed, digging deeper and deeper, the cadence picking up. Tim ejaculating again and begging for mercy, but none coming. Stroke, stroke, stroke. Thump, thump, thump.

* * * *

"Sir, sir, are you all right. Are you having a seizure of some sort? Should we call someone?"

Tim returned to full consciousness, suddenly aware that he was gripping the table top with white-knuckled fists and thumping it up and down on the brick surface of the outdoor café. The waitress also was gripping the table top, trying to hold it steady and to keep the china on top of it from tumbling to the ground.

"Sir, are you OK?" the waitress repeated. When Tim loosened his grip on the table top, so did she, and she handed forth a table check. "Sir, the older gentlemen said you'd take care of the tab for the coffees. Are you OK now?"

Tim turned his head this way and that way, fighting to bring his focus back to the sidewalk café on Wisconsin Avenue. Howard Crandal was gone from the table now—as was the handsome young man who had been so attentive at the neighboring table.

He took the check from the waitress, but he couldn't stand up for several minutes. He found that he had ejaculated in his trousers and was still half hard.

159

He looks out to the street in time to see the man with the Cavalier King spaniels rounding the corner, his back to where Tim is standing.

THE DOG GROOMER

Right off the top, I'll make quite clear that I'm not a dog person. I'm a cat person. You don't have to walk them, and they can be on their own for a weekend without chewing up the new sofa. But my wife thought we needed a dog—because we lived in a "ripe for ripping the rich folk off" golf club community, she said. But I know it was really because Libby next door got an Irish Setter, so naturally we had to have a Wolfhound.

Well, Wolfhounds are high maintenance, and I made quite clear to my wife from the get go that this was her dog. In retaliation, she decided that the dog would substitute for me everywhere except in her vagina. She still made quite clear that my cock was top dog in that kennel, but everywhere else the Wolfhound's needs came first.

And when Angie gets involved in a project, she goes the whole distance.

This is just a preamble to bringing the dog groomer on the scene. Which is what Angie did two sessions into taking Grrr (her name for the dog, not mine) to an expensive dog obedience and grooming "college." After listening to all of the introductions on how to acclimate our high-strung purebred to his home environment (presumably so he doesn't start gifting us with pungent symbols of dissatisfaction and disdain on the floor of the front foyer), Angie decided that our home had to be evaluated as to its suitability to Grrr's needs and for advice on how to bring our 4,000-square foot, $2 million hovel up to dog code. So, she paid the extra fee for the dog groomer to make a home visit and inspection.

On the appointed day, I retired to poolside in disgust, separating myself entirely from anything to do with Grrr—or my wife concerning her current project. I heard them yammering in the house, both in high-pitched voices, and I hit the pool and did enough laps that I thought I'd toned up so well on the spot that I'd just slide out of my Speedo. Then I pulled myself across the pool tiles and collapsed on the lounge bed and promptly went to sleep.

I woke to voices under the patio table umbrella nearby. Angie and the dog groomer had come out to the pool area to discuss the grim details of our home's deficiencies as a dog safe haven.

When I opened my eyes, I saw that he was staring at me— talking to Angie, but having as much attention as he could muster plastered to me as I lay there in my skimpy Speedo. I knew that look. He was interested.

I slipped my dark sunglasses on and gave him a look back. Very presentable he was. Not a pretty boy or a muscle stud by any means. But very presentable. And he had a shy look about him, which probably went over as well with the dog owners as it did with the pooches. He wasn't a limp wrister either—well, not quite—despite anything I would have assumed or because I had caught him checking my assets out, which, if I don't mind saying, were a whole bank vault full.

I watched him as he talked to Angie, and I liked his look and his manner. I could see how he'd be good at handling dogs. He showed every evidence of being good at handling people too. And the longer I watched him the more I became interested in being handled by him and handling him in turn.

Who knows who we are attracted to, what alignment of the stars and circumstance makes us want someone. I don't know and I don't care. I just know that, from that brief look at Cliff Marsden, the dog groomer, I wanted him.

And I soon could see that he felt the same way about me. He took a sudden interest in Grrr that went way beyond even Angie's interest and almost bordered on the unhealthy, I thought.

For three weeks Cliff found every form of excuse he could to drop by the house to give us this or that little thing that Grrr needed before their next grooming session or to consult with Angie on Grrr's progress in mastering good manners (which was almost nonexistent as far as I could determine). And each time, as

I saw him walking up the driveway, I found an excuse to be minimally dressed and just walking through the house wherever they were consulting. I made more trips to the front foyer in those weeks than I ever had before—and not just to clean off the inevitable present from Grrr that I usually found there. Angie, I'm sure, thought Cliff was interested in her, and she was mildly flattered. Not seriously interested, I didn't think, because Cliff's proclivities were pretty obvious and I kept Angie purring with my own attentions to her in bed. But I knew those looks he had given me. I knew when a man was interested in me.

This couldn't go on forever I thought, and Cliff was certainly playing out as the shy kind. There was nothing shy about me, though. So, I took the dog by the collar, so to speak, and made the first move myself. I set up an end-of-the-day appointment for a grooming of Grrr with Cliff. He was grooming the dogs at his home, in a downstairs room that obviously served as mud room, winter storage of the outside furniture, and laundry room—in addition to his dog work room. It was white tiled—floor, wall, and ceiling—and it looked somewhat like an operating room, with a sloping floor and drain in the center and everything. I'm sure it was ideal for whatever he had to do with the dogs, none of which I really had any interest in hearing about. I was a cat person.

"Oh, hi, Mr. Blade," he said when I arrived. "I'm surprised you came instead of Mrs. Blade. And where's Grrr?"

I just bet he was surprised to see me instead of Angie, I thought. He probably had been able to tell right off the bat, as I stretched out in feline fashion on my pool lounge bed that first day, that I was a cat person.

"I made the appointment, Cliff," I said as I moved into the room, making him retreat before me toward the alcove with the washer and dryer. "And Grrr won't be joining us either," I said.

"I don't understand. What . . .?"

"I think you'd agree that Grrr is the nervous type," I said, and then I added, a bit more maliciously than I intended, "And I think that Angie might be a bit too high strung to watch us fucking too."

163

"Excuse me, Mr. . . ." He was too shocked for words. But I was the very direct variety.

"You need no excuse, Cliff. You look just fine. And that basket of yours looks nice and bulgy too. I've seen how you look at me. Don't you think it time for you to stop making house calls and for us just to do it?"

I had him backed up against the washing machine now, and with one hand I was working the buttons on his shirt and with the other I was unbuttoning the fly to his shorts. He was stammering and yammering. But he wasn't stopping me.

I went into a lip lock while my hands ran across his body, exposing more flesh and rubbing it and gliding from one sensitive spot to another. I had him pushed into the washing machine. He was rigid at first in his confusion and not believing that this was happening so fast; not believing it was happening to him at all. But he warmed up fast enough and soon his hands were opening up and peeling away my clothing and gliding along my body as searchingly as what I was doing to him. He thawed completely to me and was devouring my mouth now and making loud, animal-like sounds.

His yammering served to summon forth a small collection of pooches, who trotted out to the grooming room from all parts of his house and politely formed a semicircle around us, making up an attentive, appreciative audience. I don't know if Cliff minded the audience, but I thought it was kind of cute. I almost wished they'd brought their wallets so I could charge admission.

We were both naked as the dogs now, if not as furry—although Cliff did have that nice chest pelt playing ring-around-a-rosy with his pert nipples, one with a silver ring in it, and trailing down his torso into his bush. I lifted him up and slammed his nicely rounded butt cheeks down on top of the washing machine and started my lips on a journey down that trail.

"Mind the machine," Cliff managed with a gasp. "It's about broke as it is."

"Oh?" I asked, suddenly quite interested. "In what way?"

"It bucks and rumbles. Practically moves across the floor."

That was good to know.

Then I continued on my tonguing journey down into the bush. Cliff gasped again when I possessed him fully with my mouth, and he made little urping sounds that had the dogs perking their ears up as I worked his cock with my lips and tongue.

All shyness was gone and he was fully into the experience now, so I pushed his back against the machine's control panel and came up on top of the machine with my knees on either side of his thighs, grasped a pipe running along the ceiling above the machine with my fists, and pushed my pelvis toward his face. Cliff got the drift of where I was going with this and worked my cock big and moist with a very soft and inviting mouth. The dogs wagged their tails, had their hinies thumping against the white tiles of the floor, and were licking their chops in empathy with the work we were doing on the washing machine. I remembered to be ever so thankful that none of them were attack dogs—Dobermans or Rottweilers—with a protective instinct for their daddy, because I was surely worrying his mouth with my poker.

When I'd worked up a good stroking rhythm of my own, I took one of my hands off the pipe and punched the washing machine button, turning it on. As Cliff had promised, it began to rumble and buck—and it added a good bounce to my fucking of his face.

He was gasping and screaming between swallows and gagging for me to fuck him for real, so I went back on my haunches a bit, pulled his legs around my hips, and drew his pelvis in toward mine. I glided inside him easily enough, which told me that this all wasn't exactly new to him and more or less assured me that he really had been signaling his want of me and was just too shy to be more direct about it. Shyness wasn't one of my problems, however.

The machine reached a particularly rumbling cycle as I bottomed out inside him, and we both had quite a long and wild ride before our own little show for the canines was over, with me spilling my seed deep inside him and him flicking his all across my belly and the top of the washing machine. I had his head flapping back and forth and his eyes wildly revolving around the grooming room and his howling setting off a chorus from our audience. All very satisfying for performers and onlookers alike.

After that I hauled him upstairs to his bedroom, laid him out on his bed on his belly ,and then laid him extra specially well and hard and deep and long. The dogs joined us on the bed, and,

165

although they didn't exactly participate in my debauching of Cliff for a second time, they certainly sat around panting as much as he did and looked very sympathetically on, probably thinking that he was in some sort of painful fix as much yelping as he was doing.

I went away with a lip-smacking appreciating for the charms of Cliff and an agreement on a time for a repeat breeding session. I made but one request—that he not get his washing machine fixed for a while. I wanted to take both it and him for a jolting ride again soon. The dogs were a good audience. But, as nice and polite and attentive as they were, I think I'm still a cat person.

THE PERSONAL ATTENDANT

He caught my eye as soon as he entered the classroom. Most of the other students were women and seemed to be comfortable with each other and their dogs. It was a night-class dog grooming class. He—his name turned out to be Cal—stuck out like a sore thumb. For one thing he was somewhat of a bruiser. He was good looking enough—in fact very good looking in a bodybuilder, square jaw, dark looks way. But he was tattooed like a biker and had that rough look about him in other ways. For another thing, he brought a large, black Poodle with him, and he handled the dog like it wasn't his and like he didn't have the foggiest idea why the Poodle had come in with him.

I didn't get a last name for him because he wasn't even registered for the class.

"Look under Jim Causey," he said when I approached him with a clipboard. I trembled a bit as I approached, because he both intimidated and aroused me. This was just the sort of man I sought out when I was between boyfriends. I was always on the lookout for a longer-termed relationship in a boyfriend, but when I was between these relationships, none of which had worked out for me, I found myself seeking out one-night stands with a brawny man. At those times I wanted a man who would manhandle me and leave me panting and moaning and unable to close my legs. I wanted to know I'd been totally fucked.

"Yes, I have a Jim Causey," I said. "Is that also you?"

He gave me a look that started mean, like he didn't like to be challenged, but then softened when it seemed like he actually looked at me for the first time. "No, that's Jim Causey rolling in now. I'm just Cal, his personal attendant."

167

"His personal attendant?" I asked, as I now saw that, indeed, a middle-aged man in a wheelchair had rolled into the classroom and moved over to the side.

"Yeah, I do pretty much everything for Mr. Causey. He's got the money to continue to live alone. And it looks like I'm going to be doing Sid for him too, just like I do him."

I took a quick look at the man in the wheelchair. He was trim despite apparently have no use of his legs. When Cal's look had softened when he gave me the once over I was sure I recognized that look. I'd gotten it often enough—the look of sexual interest. So, was he telling me that Causey was his sugar daddy? That Causey paid Cal's way and Cal took care of Causey in all ways—and of this Sid too, whoever he was?

"Doing Sid?" I asked.

"The pooch," Cal said. "This fancy dog, whatever kind it is. This is Sid."

The Poodle was crouched by Cal, looking as scared of Cal as I thought Cal had been of the dog when they came in.

"Have you handled dogs before?" I asked.

"I thought I'd handled just about everything," Cal said, giving me a searching look again—a look of checking out possibilities?—"but I ain't ever done a dog before."

The first thing that came to mind was, well, that's good. You could go to jail for doing a dog. I nearly laughed at that, but then it struck me that Cal presented just like the inmates had in the special class I'd taught at a prison, a vocational class in giving inmates skills they could use on the outside. A slightly touchy demeanor with more than a touch of challenge and bad ass to it.

"You sure you want to do this, then?"

"You teachin' the class?" he asked.

"Yes."

"Then I want to do this." I took that as confirmation of his interest—but maybe more in me than the class. I wondered if his sugar daddy knew he was on the make with other men. It sort of gave me a jolt, though, that it might be me. He was just the kind of bruiser I was in the mood for—in a temporary, one-night way. Or one afternoon. Or just a half hour on top of the table here after the rest of the class had left.

Cal surprised me in the class. He had an intimidating demeanor and big hands, but his hands weren't clumsy, and over the two-hour class both he and Sid became comfortable with each other. Sid seemed apprehensive about the whole situation, but the dog was thoroughly cowed by Cal, and when Cal put his hands on the dog and moved it into this position or that as the grooming required, the dog obeyed. It would be skittish right up until Cal put his hands on it and then it would settle down, trembling slightly.

I trembled slightly myself at seeing Cal do that, and I'll readily admit that I thought of the big bruiser of a tattooed man doing that to me as well. He was prime one-night-stand material.

Jim Causey didn't just sit back and watch during the session. He was right up there with Cal, watching his every move and giving him encouragement and talking to the dog. The two men obviously had a relationship going, one that I envied.

"You got dogs too?" Cal asked me near the end of the class.

"Yes," I answered. "I have a few Maltese. I show those. I have a Poodle bitch too. Smaller than Sid. I don't show her, but I breed her. She's good stock."

"Seems strange to have those two kinds, even if both are of the limp-wristed variety," he said. "Aren't Maltese a yappy little dog. And Poodles—"

"Maltese can be a bit yappy, yes, but Poodles are smart dogs. The breed started out as hunting dogs," I answered, resisting noting that he himself had come in with a Poodle. "The Poodle was left behind after a relationship that went bad. I didn't mind. I liked the dog much more than I liked him." I nearly froze when the "him" came out. I was revealing more than I had intended to.

I looked up to see a slight smirk on Cal's face. "I knew I was right," he said in a low voice.

I just blushed. There didn't seem to be anything to say to either try to cover up or expand on the slip about having had a relationship with a male.

"Know a good place to exercise them on Saturday mornings?" he asked, smoothly switching gears. "I don't like the thought of Sid being cooped up all the time. He's a big dog; he needs to be able to run regularly. All big animals need to be able to run free, to do what they like as long as it don't hurt no one else."

I felt a bit of a chill going up my back, my first thought being of a hunk like him running free—running naked and then doing what he wanted. Maybe to me. I tried to concentrate on the canine aspect of what he'd said. I was surprised that he showed such concern for the dog and, before thinking better of it, said so.

"No one—man nor animal—should be cooped up," he repeated, with an edge of vehemence. "It just ain't right."

This only made me think again about that class I taught at the prison.

"I take my dogs to West Side Park occasionally on Saturday mornings," I answered. "They have an off-the-leash area at that time."

"You'll be there next Saturday?"

"I suppose I might."

"And you'll bring the Poodle bitch." It didn't sound like a question.

One of the other students broke in to ask a question before I could answer or ask about that, and when I finished talking to her, Cal was wheeling Jim Causey out of the room, with Sid trotting beside him, both Cal and the dog seeming much less skittish than when they'd come into the classroom.

I went home humming. I don't know whether it was because I considered any class where a master and dog had melded as well as Cal and Sid had was a victory or if it was because Cal was my ideal image of a one-night stand and had shown interest in me.

I didn't, of course, have any intention of going to the park with Starbright, the zany name my spaced-out, once-significant other had tagged the Poodle bitch with, but almost like a zombie, I loaded her up and drove out to the park on Saturday morning.

Cal and Sid were there, in West Park, Sid already off the leash and running around the dog run area, when we arrived. We were the only ones who showed up.

The day was hot, the sun beating down on us, and I found Cal sitting on a blanket under some trees at the verge of the meadow Sid was cavorting in. He was wearing shorts and sandals. He'd taken off his T-shirt. My impression that he was a bodybuilder was borne out by his muscular and cut torso. The tattooing I had seen running up his arms continued on the chest and back and down onto his legs in a riot of color.

"Let her off the leash and sit down here with me," he said when I arrived.

It no longer was the teacher, me, giving instruction to him. He was in command. I fell right in with this change. It was, after all, what I had dreamed of in the four days since the class, while all along I was telling myself I wouldn't show up on Saturday—that he had my telephone number through the school and could pursue me a bit if he really was interested.

But I wasn't kidding myself. I knew all along that if he wanted me, he could have me, and that I melted to a man who took control. This, I was only beginning to realize, was the problem with the long-term boyfriends I had tried. They related to me as equals and all were attentive to my needs. That was all well and fine, but it paled when we got down to the sex act against my arousal to a man who just took me because he wanted me—and who had the cock to keep me pinned down and panting.

I let Starbright off the leash, and she took off into the meadow and was tearing around with Sid in no time at all.

I sat down beside Cal, and he leaned in close to me. We spoke for a few minutes about I knew not what—something to do with the class and pointers he wanted to understand better. It was just nervous small talk—on my part at least. I kept looking around for other dogs and owners to show up, but none did. Cal didn't seem nearly as nervous as I was. He just crept closer until he had an arm around me.

I couldn't even have told where the transition was in his putting his hands on me—in a possessive way—pulling my T-shirt over my head, and turning my mouth to his for a controlling kiss that took my breath away. I was trembling at the strong grip of his hand on my waist and then inner thigh, and then cock. He was stroking me hard and still possessing me with a kiss, and I was breathing hard. It was all him, controlling me. Just as I wanted in a one-night stand.

When we pulled out of the kiss, with me already pulled over into his lap and able to feel the insistent hardness of him, I looked out into the meadow.

171

Starbright was standing perfectly still and Sid had mounted her and was breeding her.

"Look, Cal, we've got to stop that!" I cried, struggling to get up. But Cal was holding me fast in his lap.

"Let them have their fun. She obviously wants it," Cal answered. "All creatures should be free to do what makes them happy. Just like you and I are gonna do. You see that. See how big and pink that stud's cock is? I'm gonna do you just like Sid is doin' that bitch of yours. I'm going to fuck you, aren't I?"

I didn't deny that he was. I just moaned.

He pushed me forward on all fours then, pulled my shorts down low on my thighs, had his cock out and crowned, and mounted and slid into me. I moaned and groaned as he became fully saddled. He held there, not moving, but deeply sheathed, until I started panting hard and begging him to fuck me. Then he laughed and set the cock in motion, fucking me hard and deep as we watched Sid breeding Starbright.

I breathed hard but held steady, just as Starbright did, knowing full well that this was exactly what I wanted, a hard-bodied man who knew who he was and what he wanted, moving a long, thick cock inside me. Taking me roughly, naturally, fully, in total control.

* * * *

I was panting hard, lying on my back at the edge of my bed, with Cal between my thighs, holding my legs up and out, his pelvis making rapid undulations as he fucked me. I had already come, spouting up onto my belly, and he was working on it. He was looking intensely down into my face, but I was watching the play of his tattoos with the expanding and contracting of the muscles of his chest during his exertions. He was deep inside me, throbbing and pistoning me. I contracted the muscles of my channel in his cock, arched my back, and cried out "Now, now, now!"

I could feel him jerk and come, filling out the bulb of the condom. He pulled out of me immediately and turned and sat on the bed next to me. My own legs reached for the floor at the foot of the bed. He looked down at me and gave me a smirk.

"That was good. I like what you did there—to make me come." He bent down, messed around in the pockets of the trousers he'd dropped on the floor below the bed, and came up with a pack of cigarettes and some matches. He lit up, sitting there, legs spread and elbows on knees, and inhaled and exhaled a couple of times. My instinct was to make a comment about the cancer he was exhaling into the air in my place with that smoke, but I didn't say anything. It all went with the package that made me melt to him.

He'd left me there on the ground Saturday morning, just two days earlier, zipping up his shorts and padding out onto the field to retrieve Sid, who had also finished breeding Starbright. Hadn't said a thing. He'd taken hold of me and fucked me as naturally as Sid had mounted Starbright—just like it was the most natural thing to do. No emotional entanglements at all. Knowing that I wanted him and would just hold steady on all fours while he breeded me too.

I sat up half dazed, but well fucked, and watched him go to the parking lot, get into a black Escalade that had been parked there when I drove in in my Camaro, and peel out of the park. I thought that would be the last I'd see of him, him fulfilling my idea of a tough-guy one-night stand.

The first thing I'd done when I got home was to go online trying to find the pedigree of his Poodle. It hadn't been that zany that I'd let him fuck me in the park. I had practically rolled over and begged for it back in class. What had been zany was letting his dog fuck mine. I bred her for the money her pedigree pups brought in. I found, though, that the lines for Jim Causey's Poodle were as good as Starbright's own, so I wasn't fucked there, if the breeding had taken. I'd saved a stud fee.

I thought briefly that I should have paid Cal a stud fee because he had taken care of me so well. I almost regretted that he was one-night-stand material.

But then I'd answered a ring at the door of my house on Tuesday afternoon, and there he was.

"Been thinkin' of you since Saturday," he said.

I looked past him to the driveway. He was driving a beat-up old Dodge Ram today. I decided the Escalade must have been Jim Causey's car.

"I didn't expect to see you again," I said.

"I didn't expect it either," he replied.

"So," I said.

"So, do you want me to fuck you here in the doorway, or do you have a bed?"

When he put it that way, how could I refuse? We kissed and groped each other in my bedroom, at the foot of my bed. The dogs had watched us with curiosity as he followed me through the house to the bedroom, but I shut them out. They were used to watching my boyfriends fuck me, but that had never been rough play. I expected this to be rough, and I didn't want any of them to get the wrong idea and to take a chunk out of Cal's buttocks when I was screaming and squirming under him.

He had pushed me down hard on the foot of the bed with a shove of the heel of his hand to my sternum, and I'd watched him strip his clothes off. I was just wearing shorts, and he had no trouble jerking them and my briefs off my legs. He was more than half hard. And, with him, half hard was breathtakingly enough.

With no discussion or preliminaries of any type, he came up on the bed, straddled my chest; grabbed my wrists with his fists, forcing my arms above my head and wide; and arched his chest over my head, pressing the bulb of his cock at my lips. I opened my mouth to him, and he face fucked me, making me gag and groan while he stroked and filled out.

Again, without saying anything, he moved right into crouching between my thighs, with one hand on my throat, holding me to the bed, and the fingers of the other one opening my channel up with the help of spit. My legs were running up his chest. I was gasping for breath, my eyes bugging out, and staring into his face. He let loose of my throat and pulled his fingers out of my hole, grabbed my ankles, raised and jerked my legs painfully spread wide, and went right to fucking me. I had no idea when he'd rolled the condom on.

He fucked me hard, forcing himself right inside me and pistoning hard and deep. He pumped my legs back and forth, in to his hips and then brutally wide out as he punched his cock up into me, to the rhythm of his stroke. I jerked and grunted, my torso coming off the surface of the bed with each thrust, and I wondered if I'd be able to walk the next day. But I didn't care. I was vocal enough that the dogs were barking and scratching at the bedroom door. I was glad I'd closed them out.

"Do you always fuck this way?" I asked him after he was done and was sitting on the edge of the bed, smoking a cigarette, as I lay behind him, my arm around his waist, my hand encasing the root of his cock.

"You learn to be quick about it in prison. It goes on all over the place, but mostly on the sly."

I nearly gasped. I wasn't surprised, but I wasn't prepared to have been right.

He turned toward me and leaned over, his eyes searching my face for my reaction to that revelation. I reached up with a hand and traced the tattooing on his chest.

"Is that where you got the tattoos too?"

"You have plenty of time to collect those in prison," he answered.

"How long have you been out?"

"Two months. I was in more for who I was associated with than for what I did."

"And Jim Causey waited for you?"

"Just hooked up with him. He's my work release arrangement. I'm his personal attendant. Like I told you."

"I thought he was your sugar daddy or something. That personal attendant was something very personally applied."

"I don't fuck him, if that's what you mean. I jack him off when he needs it and let him blow me when he wants."

Somehow I didn't see the difference. Causey kept him for sex.

"Look. He was the work release situation I was assigned to for my probation."

"And you take care of all of his personal needs, plus you groom his Poodle for him."

"The grooming was part of the deal. I have to do community service for six months, while I'm on probation. Causey hooked me up with a no-kill dog rescue center. I can do my community service by grooming dogs there. He said it would be one of the easier ways to do community service and it seems right to me. I'd rather deal with pooches than with people. I haven't been very good in dealing with people."

175

"But Causey would like you to stay on with him after the six months, I'll bet, and I'll also bet that you're willing to do that."

"Listen, I came here to fuck, not to play twenty questions. You tired of doin' that? I have other places I could be."

"You know I'm not tired of it—well, I am; you've worn me out. But that doesn't mean I want it to stop. But you don't have to leave at all. I can offer you the same deal as Causey is doing for this six months. I can hook you up with dog grooming credits for community service. You can be *my* personal attendant."

"I can attend you right now," he growled. "Pull up onto the bed on your belly."

I did so as he put his cigarette out in an ashtray on the nightstand and rolled on another condom.

Once more he showed me both that he didn't much care for conversation and that I was weak enough to take his fucking anyway I could get it, as he straddled my buttocks, slid back into me, and, leaning his chest over my back with his weight on the heels of hands placed on either side of my shoulders, began to pump me hard and deep again.

After he'd ejaculated again, I was still so half blotto from the hard fucking he'd given me that I just laid there and watched him light up the cigarette again and then, when he'd finished it, pull on his shorts and sandals and move over to and open the bedroom door. My dogs rushed right past him to ensure I was OK, and by the time I got them off me, he was gone.

And he was gone for six months. He not only had doubled the one-night stands I had with big, dominating bruisers like him, but he also had taken a chunk of my heart. Maybe one night was all I could afford with someone like him. Perhaps I grew too attached to and needy for men who could give me what Cal did. Anyway I moped for a couple of months, tried to forget about him for a couple of months, and slowly was on the way to do so for a couple of months.

Starbright moped too. Nothing came of Sid's studding of her in the park.

* * * *

I'd like to say I'd forgotten Cal by six months later, but I hadn't. I'd cruised around a bit and also tried out another live-in of the domestic variety, but whenever I was with any of these guys, I was thinking of Cal and comparing them to him—and they all were coming up short.

So, imagine my surprise when the doorbell rang and Starbright barked and came to the door with me, with her tongue hanging out. I was surprised because she had never shown this much interest in anyone being at the front door before.

It was Cal. And not just Cal; Sid was sitting at his side, tail wagging to beat the band.

"Six months are up. You still have an opening for a personal attendant?" he asked.

"What happened with Jim Causey?" I asked.

"Nothing happened. And that's sort of the point," Cal said. "I was assigned to him for six months and the six months are up. I'm off probation. I sort of like grooming the dogs at the no-kill pound. If you don't mind, I'll continue that."

"If I don't mind?"

"Yeah, if you want me to live with you and do you right."

Want him to live with me? Of course I did. I hadn't even thought hard on that until now, and when it came up just now I realized this was what I needed all along. I didn't need a limp-wristed guy to take care of me. I needed someone like Cal for me to take care of—whenever he wasn't taking care of me sexually.

"I don't understand," I said, still not believing him just showing up again after six months. "I offered you this six months ago."

"Yeah, you did. But I had a commitment to Causey. He was taking a chance on me. The shrink in prison told me that what I needed to do to stay out of trouble was to make commitments and stick with them. I did that with Causey. I want to try doing that with you now."

"But Sid, here. You brought Causey's dog with you."

"Turns out Sid likes me a lot better than he likes Causey, so we got him a Rin Tin Tin-type dog. I'm banking on you being happy with Sid doing your Poodle as good as I can do you."

I looked down at Starbright. She certainly was acting like she wanted Sid to do her again.

"Maybe I'll let them socialize out in the fenced backyard" I said.

"While you're taking them back, I'll be waiting in your bedroom," he said.

And as simple as that, I at last got the ultimate live-in arrangement—and my own very personal attendant to boot.

~

ABOUT THE AUTHOR

Habu is one of the pen names of a former supersonic spy jet pilot, intelligence agent, male model, movie actor, and diplomat. A wild youth in South East Asia was spent enjoying whatever sexual opportunities came his way, and much of his gay male writing is about recalling incidents from those days and inventing ones he'd perhaps have liked to experience. He now leads a very quiet and ordinary happily married family life.

An American, he is a published mainstream novelist and short story writer under another name and in another dimension of his life. He has written or cowritten (with Sabb) approaching 1,000 published short stories and over 100 published erotica e-books, primarily of gay fiction but also memoir, straight fiction and ménage fiction. His hand and creative writing can be seen in stories and books by habu, sr71plt, Dirk Hessian, Shabbu, and Stephen Kessel—among unrevealed others that might surprise readers. The fictionalized GM memoir *Flying High, Diving Deep* is loosely based on his life experiences. He can be found at the adults only gay male site www.BarbarianSpy.com, which he shares with Sabb and Dirk Hessian.

Our authors always like to receive feedback, and appreciate it when readers post reviews at distributors and other review sites.

BarbarianSpy

FOR LITERARY HEAT

Not all books listed below may currently be on release.
* indicates the book is available in paperback and e-book.

BOOKS BY DIRK HESSIAN
Xtreme Erotica
The King's Men
Shores of Tripoli
Prophecy of Noto
Pretender's Fate
General Erotica/Romance
Fire Down the Valley*
Constantinople*
The Beautiful Way*
Blue and Gray
Colonel's Treasure
Beginning of Time
Labyrinth
BOOKS BY HABU
Gay Erotica
Memoir Faction
Flying High, Diving Deep*
Xtreme Erotica
Apyko: The Greek Pimp
Visits of the Schlange
Second Coming: Emile La Cour Unleashed
Vortex: Sacrificed by Curiosity*
Dark Angel Sounding (in e-book & included in
Sounding:Ultimate Control Paperback)*
Sounding: Ultimate Control (Print Only)*
Sounding Five (in e-book & included in Sounding:Ultimate
Control paperback)*
General Erotica

Romance
Ravens Roost
Caribbean Cruise Top to Bottom
Arena Stage
Trading Partners (Valentine's Day)
Friday Nights with Lenny (Christmas Romance)
Snowy, Snowy Nights (Christmas Romance)
Four Coins
Lower Than the Heart (Valentine's Day)
Brambleton
Gotta Keep Trying
Finding Amnad
Platres Conclave
Other Novels/Novellas
Stallion Station
Racing With the Devil (espionage suspense)
Cruising Gigolo (bisexual)
Prepared in Cape Verdi
Gilded Cage
House on Park
Anything for Ambition
Dance of the Ravishers
Hard Knocks U*
My Neighbor's Spa*
Man's Man: Tales of a High Priced Gay Hooker*
Trip Money
Clint Folsom Mysteries Compendium Volume 1*
Death to Blonds - Stolen Judgment (Clint Folsom Mystery)*
Clint Folsom Mysteries Compendium Volume 2*
The Indian Doctor
Sailorboy
Home to Fire Island
Choke Hold
Gay Erotica Anthologies
Eleven to the Dogs
Fifty Seventy*
Spy Tails 001*

Spy Tails 002*
Doubled*
Doubled Again*
Tails in the Tropics*
Tails in the Med*
Tails in the West*
Rough Riders*
Grab Bag 1*
Grab Bag 2*
Grab Bag 3*
Grab Bag 4*
Grab Bag 5*
Beyond the Beaded Curtain*
Habu's Christmas Balls
The Sporting Life*
Fetish Galore!*
Literary Gay Erotica
Cairo Surrender*
The Handyman*
Homeward Bound
Journey to Mirage*
Menage Erotica
Cruising Gigolo
13 Ways for Halloween
Luther*
The Indian Prince
Literary GLBT Fiction
Summer of Denial
BOOKS BY SHABBU
Velvet Interrogation
Finding Jason
Dirty Pool
Operation Black Jade
Cigars!*
Angel in the Barn
Gayly Complicated*
Despoiling David
The Tree of Idleness*

I Met a Man
Rough Road to Happiness
BOOKS BY SABB
Hiring in Hollywood
The Legend of Holleystone Grange
Surprise Encounters
She is He
Wrong Man
Loyal to his King
Barbarian Tales - Book One - Traveler's Tales*
Barbarian Tales - Book Two - Journeys Begin*
Barbarian Tales - Book Three - The Inheritance*
Barbarian Tales - Book Four - Road to Persepolis*

www.ingramcontent.com/pod-product-compliance
Lightning Source LLC
Chambersburg PA
CBHW020124180626
46810CB00004B/1398

* 9 7 8 0 9 8 7 6 0 9 3 8 0 *